SUCCUBUS SINS

USA TODAY BESTSELLING AUTHOR

J.R. THORN

Author's Note

Welcome to the series that started it all... The Blood Stone Series!

I started my journey writing reverse harem with Sonya's struggle. My muse rarely listens to me, so when Sonya began to take more than one mate, I was confused, but not concerned, given that she's a succubus. Because of Sonya's story, I stepped into reverse harem and now over 14 books later, I haven't looked back!

I know that I have a large catalogue, so if you are looking for my latest work that represents my current level as an established author, I suggest reading Elemental Fae Academy or Fortune Academy. An author naturally progresses over time, so my older work like Succubus Sins is going to be a bit more raw and complex, but it's one of my favorite series. Don't expect a cookie-cutter story with Sonya and her mates!

Some triggers to be aware of for reverse harem readers, not all love interests make it into the harem. There is a satisfactory ending, but not all plot loops are closed because Seven Sins is part of a massive shared world, so you need to keep reading the next series to find out what happens with some characters.

This is a fast-burn reverse harem romance. Mature scenes include F/F, F/F/M, F/M/M, and F/M. Two of the four-man harem are introduced in Book 1 with the the rest of the relationships developing through books 2 and 3.

Thank you for walking with me on this journey. I hope you enjoy it!

XOXO

Succubus Sins © 2018 by J.R. Thorn
ISBN: 9781794556966

Cover Art by Sanja Balan
Line-Editing by Kristen Breanne

RECOMMENDED READING ORDER

All Books are Standalone Series listed by their
sequential order of events

Elemental Fae Universe Reading List

- Elemental Fae Academy: Books 1-3 (Co-Authored)

- Midnight Fae Academy (Lexi C. Foss)

- Fortune Fae Academy (J.R. Thorn)

- Fortune Fae M/M Steamy Episodes (J.R. Thorn)

- Candela (J.R. Thorn)

- Winter Fae Queen (Co-Authored)

- Hell Fae (Co-Authored)

Blood Stone Series Universe Reading List

Recommended Reading Order is Below

Seven Sins

- *Book 1: Succubus Sins*

- *Book 2: Siren Sins*

- *Book 3: Vampire Sins*

The Vampire Curse: Royal Covens

- *Book 1: Her Vampire Mentors*

- *Book 2: Her Vampire Mentors*

- *Book 3: Her Vampire Mentors*

Fortune Academy (Part I)

- *Year One*

- *Year Two*

- *Year Three*

Fortune Academy Underworld (Part II)

- *Episode 1: Burn in Hell*

- *Book Four*

- *Book Five*

- *Book Six*

Fortune Academy Underworld (Part III)

- *Book Seven*

- *Book Eight*

- *Book Nine*

Crescent Five *(Rejected Mate Wolf Shifter RH)*

• *Book One: Moon Guardian*

• *Book Two*

• *Book Three*

Dark Arts Academy (Vella)

Ongoing serial

Unicorn Shifter Academy

• *Book One*

• *Book Two*

• *Book Three*

Non-RH Books (J.R. Thorn writing as Jennifer Thorn)

Noir Reformatory Universe Reading List

Noir Reformatory: The Beginning

Noir Reformatory: First Offense

Noir Reformatory: Second Offense

Noir Reformatory Turns RH from this point with the addition of a third mate

Noir Reformatory: Third Offense

Sins of the Fae King Universe Reading List

(Book 1) Captured by the Fae King

(Book 2) Betrayed by the Fae King

Learn More at www.AuthorJRThorn.com

CHAPTER 1

SEVEN
DEADLY
SINS

*D*arkness has chased me all my life. It's not tangible, and Sarah thinks it was all in my head, but the painful seven runes on my stomach aren't part of my imagination. Four of them cluster together around my navel, each with a distinct pattern as if representing a different piece of my soul. Three more runes wander on the outside, only one glowing with a soft pink of satisfaction and giving me enough power to stay alive. I feel like if I'd never met Sarah, I most certainly would have died.

Even now, as I lay awake in my bed with

Sarah sleeping peacefully at my side, I run my fingers over the slightly raised scars. They hum with a need I can't explain. Anyone lucky enough to have seen them thinks they're tattoos, but I was born with them. The top one just above my navel has a maddening itch and my nails go to it, softly scratching, which doesn't award me with any relief. I don't want to turn on the lights and look at it. I know it's only getting worse, darker and angrier as if I am supposed to be doing something to stop the darkness from coming. It's trying to urge me, but to do what... I don't know. My heart quickens with fear. If I don't figure out what it means soon... the darkness will find me. Of that much I'm sure.

The rune. I feel like it's supposed to help me, but at the same time, I know that it's a beacon to a force I can't even begin to describe. I've seen it in my dreams. I don't dare close my eyes and face the nightmares again. When I do, dark claws rake the skies of my dreams. It's a horrifying cloud of glittering blackness and it's coming after me. It's always been coming after me, but now time is running short. The edges of my vision are weakening, and no matter how many times I rub my eyes, I can't shake the feeling that I'm slowly dying and the rest of the world will come tumbling after me.

SUCCUBI DEN

*S*leep so wasn't happening and there was one thing worse than an insatiable itch across my abdomen, and that was the gnawing hunger that was making me see red. I found myself wandering the streets heading to the one place that could offer some small sense of relief to a succubus such as myself. If I didn't get the sexual nourishment I needed soon, I *would* die. It was kind of ironic. A part of me felt like I was meant to be loyal to a select few, yet my nature compelled me to seek nourishment and filled me with a lustful need that pushed away any rationalization. My fingers slipped under the low hem of my shirt and scratched at the blasted runes that wouldn't leave me alone with their incessant itching. I cast a glance at the sky, almost expecting the claws from my nightmares to streak through the low, sleepy clouds and come after me, but nothing happened.

Even if the nightmares were all in my head, I was still a succubus, and the starvation I'd been subjecting myself to was very real, and very dangerous. Sarah would find me in the afterlife and kill me all over again if I allowed myself to starve when all this time she was convinced that she could satiate my magical, sexual nourishment needs.

The last place in the world I wanted to be was a slum like Seattle's Succubi Den. The tattered awning peeked through the foggy horizon surrounded by slanted buildings. Approaching it, I pulled my hoodie closer around my face, but my sensual gait betrayed what I was. I couldn't hide my nature, and I hated how I was growing nauseatingly accustomed to handing over a hundred dollar bill to a round-faced succubus who leaned over a polished counter.

Fucking paying for it. So humiliating.

She'd started the business to help succubi and incubi who'd run into unique difficulties with their life-sucking magic, but finding enough willing participants to donate their life-force didn't come for free. She probably thought I was sick, because I kept coming back. Sometimes the magical wells got clogged, be it a magical manifestation or an emotional one. We needed sex to survive, or at least we needed to feed off sexual energy. Pain tingled along my fingertips and was the first warning sign that I was getting close to my own mortal limit of enduring abstinence.

"Why do you keep coming back, hun?" the succubus named Lucy asked with a concerned knit to her brow. She gave me a once-over, noting my fingers still under my shirt scratching away like some kind of drug addict. Aside from my quirks, I was the perfect succubus. Her eyes roamed over my voluptuous boobs that only got in the way, and noted my plump lips. She sighed. "I know there's nothing wrong with your magic. I just can't work out why you need a Den."

I glared at her until she produced a golden key to my assigned bedroom. It was none of her business. When I took the key, I decided to humor her this time. Maybe she'd understand. "I've got a girlfriend," I muttered.

She painted on a fake smile, but homosexuality in the succubi community was widely frowned upon. I didn't expect judgment from a do-gooder like Lucy, but there was pity in her eyes.

By our nature, we could only feed on those of the opposite sex. To maintain a relationship with a same-sex partner was both unfair and unsatisfactory on both sides. Most succubi enjoyed the occasional orgy or threesome, but a one-on-one relationship with a same-sex partner just wasn't done, even in a community designed around sex.

"That's a shame," she said as I walked away. "We have a program for that."

Bristling, I shot back, "I don't need fixing. I just need breakfast."

"Well hello again, sweetheart," a handsome incubus greeted me as he lewdly stretched over silk bedsheets. I didn't know his name, and I wanted to keep it that way. All I needed to know was that he had enough power to keep me alive without making me break my promise to Sarah.

A hundred dollars bought me ten minutes

with the den's most powerful incubi, and even if ten minutes wasn't much, it was all I needed not to fall over and wither into a pile of Sonya-shaped dirt.

Without wasting time, I crawled over him and bit his lip hard enough to make him flinch. "No talking," I reminded him of our golden rule. It was bad enough that I had to do this. I wanted to get what I needed, and then get out of here, wiping my memory clean as best I could.

As his hands wrapped around my hips and grated me over his stiffening erection, separating us only by a thin layer of sheets and my own clothes, his fingers squeezed as I began the feed.

The soft magic of his life-force bled into me and I gasped with slight relief. Knocking my head back, my eyes fluttered closed as he kissed his way down my neck and peeled away my shirt. I flinched when his fingers ran over the raised scar of my runes and I pushed his hands away. He wasn't allowed to touch me there. Something deep within me knew that those runes weren't meant for him. He obeyed, his touch and kisses going to the soft skin of my neck and the taut skin around my thighs. Numbness fled from my extremities and a satisfying warmth curled in my belly. The itch from my rune still persisted, but at least it was more manageable when I had the energy to ignore it.

"It's been months of foreplay," he complained. "You only tease me, succubus."

I jerked and wrapped my fingers around his neck. He only grinned at my anger. "I said no talking."

He offered me a slow nod of agreement and shifted me over him, rubbing through my jeans with his erection that was now in full force.

His arousal gave me a surplus of energy and what I couldn't feed on filtered through the air in an unused hint of sweat and sex. I wanted to go farther, to give into the temptation to sheath him and ride out this aching need inside of me. I could survive with these snacks, but every time, I grew just a little bit weaker when I denied a climax my body craved.

"I see it in your eyes," he purred, his grin coming back to taunt me. "You're going to need to feed soon, really feed, not just these little snacks, and if you don't give in, you're going to harm yourself." He lifted me with an ease that pissed me off. He flipped me on my back and gave me a deep kiss. Part of me wanted to toss him off, but I reminded myself that I was still halfway clothed. I was still protected by fabric that stretched its restriction across my hips and kept him from pushing me to do something I knew I'd regret.

When he went for my zipper, I snatched his fingers in the strongest grip I could manage. "No," I told him. "You know the rules."

He sighed, because even if he was a powerful incubus, I was still his client. "Very well," he said, and leaned in to graze his lips across my neck. "When you're ready, I'll be here, and what you really need will be on the house."

*S*hivering, even though Seattle was humidly hot during the day, I wrapped my fingers around my elbows and marched away from Seattle's Succubi Den as the sun banished most of the fog. This was the moment I painfully wiped away my memories of kisses and teasing at the hands of an incubus I'd paid to be with. Sarah didn't know, couldn't know, that I had to resort to a Den to stay alive.

She believed that I could feed on her, and because she was a muse, she was strong enough to survive me.

I couldn't tell her the truth. Not yet.

But this time, the need inside of me hadn't relaxed. I'd banished only the worst of the pains that came with starvation from abstinence. But even though I still tasted the musky delight of an incubus on my lips, he'd been right. I couldn't keep this up for much longer. I doubled over when my rune changed its reminder from an itch to a stab of pain, just like I'd been gouged by a blade. I groaned and lifted my shirt, cursing when a drop of blood squeezed from the center of the rune that had turned so black it was in danger of scabbing over.

"Damn it," I spat, and marched back home towards Sarah.

What the fuck was I going to do now?

HOME SWEET HOME

Sarah wasn't home when I returned, which wasn't until the day was almost over. Let her think I went to work. That sounded a lot less pathetic than wandering Seattle trying to get an incubus' sex scent off my body.

"Sonya!" Sarah squealed as she burst through the door. A sports tank clung to her sweat-glistened body and she wrapped her arms around my neck. I smiled against her teeth as she gave me a sweet kiss. She leaned and gave me a smug grin. She knew the effect she had on me made me crazy. "What's for dinner?" she asked.

I gave her a raised brow. "Pizza?"

She laughed with delight. "Perfect!"

"Didn't you just work out?" I asked as I poked her perfectly flexed abdomen.

She smirked and detached herself from me before waltzing down the hall. "Working out is just so I can eat all the pizza I want, duh." She gave me a wink over her shoulder before she disappeared upstairs. I stared after her until the sounds of a shower running intertwined with the pounding of my heart.

I loved life with Sarah, at least when it was like this. She was always happy and giggling, and a little hole inside of me welled with guilt knowing that I was lying to her. If the truth came out, she'd be broken.

That guilt nagged at me as I slumped on the couch and flipped open the laptop to order pizza.

I picked out our standard, two medium pizzas and a liter of soda, but just as I hit the confirm button, tiny zaps jolted up my fingertips. I hissed and tried to make a fist, but a fresh jolt of pain went through my temple and I jerked, sending the laptop careening to the floor. "Damn it!" I yelled as the screen swept with white lines before losing power altogether. Sarah and I were both bartenders, and even though we were both holding Seattle's record for tips per night, things were running tight. Sarah didn't know that half my tips were going to a Den's incubus down the street. I couldn't explain why I couldn't afford to fix a laptop.

Sarah rushed to the top of the stairs with wet strands of hair clinging to her face and a towel clutched to her chest. It twisted, in danger of falling off her body. "Babe, you okay?"

She frowned as I swayed on my feet. "I'm—" I tried to say, but the world spun and the next thing I knew Sarah was screaming my name as I fell into the cackling blackness of my nightmares.

*W*hen I finally awoke, it was to Sarah's deep frown. She towered over me and tiny droplets fell from her curls. Okay, that was a good sign. I hadn't been out long. "You had me worried sick!" she snapped.

I gave her a wry smile. "You're going to give yourself wrinkles with a frown like that," I croaked.

Unamused, she gave me a nudge. "The hell is going on?" She surveyed me, as if looking for what had caused my episode. "I didn't think succubi were supposed to get sick."

Easing up, I clutched my pounding head and ignore the urge to scratch the enflamed rune at the apex of my stomach. I didn't want to admit what was wrong. I hadn't had sex with a male in six months and my body was starting to rebel. I couldn't keep this up for much longer. "It's nothing," I murmured.

Her frown deepened with a vengeance. "Don't make me read your mind. Because I will!"

Black dots sprinkled across my vision as I forced myself to stand. Sarah shot up to guide me, still only wearing her pink towel.

"Don't threaten me with your mighty muse ways," I teased and pinched her chin. "I'm just hungry, that's all."

She narrowed her eyes. "But we just had sex last night." She pouted. "Am I starting to bore you?"

I huffed a laugh and kissed her cheek. "Of course not, my beautiful girlfriend. I'm just having trouble feeding. I'll go see a doctor first thing in the morning."

She frowned. "A doctor, or a *doctor* doctor?"

I snickered. "What other kind of doctor is there?"

She frowned. "There are doctors, and then there are those creepster voodoo witches you call succubi doctors. I don't trust them." She turned over her palms and looked into them as if she could read her own future. By the lines on her face, she didn't like what she saw. "They'll tell you that you need a boyfriend."

Easing back down to her side, I took her face in my hands. "That's not going to happen, okay? I'd rather die than cheat on you."

Her glittering eyes found mine, instantly glassy with emotion. As a muse, Sarah could be extreme when it came to passion, but that's what I loved about her. "Then prove them wrong. Feed on me, and don't hold back."

She pressed her warm lips to mine and the sweetness of her magic filled my senses. I couldn't feed on her, no matter how much I wished I could, but there was so much power that her presence still made me drunk. I didn't fake the impact she had on me.

"We don't need to—" I began to protest.

Sarah eased her fingers over my breast and

nipped my lip with her teeth, making me flinch. She licked over the small hurt. "You need to feed. I'm always hot for you, babe. Take what you need from me."

I needed to feed, and as much as Sarah aroused me, and I aroused her, sex with her wouldn't fix what was wrong with me. "Okay," I said with a grin, in spite of the emptiness of her offer to most succubi. "But the pizza guy is going to be here soon and I'm not going to fuck you through dinner again."

She sighed and pressed herself to me, fitting her curves perfectly into mine. "We'll see about that." She flashed me a smile that was full of mischief and tugged me to the stairs. "I still need to finish my shower."

Reluctantly I allowed Sarah to drag me through our bedroom and into the confined space of our apartment's stand-up shower. She curled her fingers under my shirt and I lifted my arms to allow her to peel it off. She glanced at my angry runes. She ran a finger around the top one that had turned black. "Is that normal?"

I grabbed her fingers and brought them up to my lips for a kiss. The worry lines across her face smoothed as she smiled. She knew I didn't like to talk about it, and she appeased me, giving me what we both wanted instead.

This was what I enjoyed with Sarah. She was so strong and dominant. I never got to experience that with men who were enthralled to me the moment I even thought about spreading my legs. But Sarah? I could never tell her no, and it felt nice to be wanted for me instead of my magic.

After I'd stepped out of my jeans, I squeezed into the shower with Sarah and wrapped my arms around her. I smiled as she kissed my neck. I squeezed her perfectly formed butt cheeks in return. "You're working out too much," I teased. "I think you could open a beer bottle with these."

She growled as she slid her fingers into me, sending my breath hitching. "You don't want to tease me," she warned. "I'll make you suffer and then we'll miss dinner for good."

I rolled my eyes into the back of my head as pleasure wafted through me. When I gave in and moaned, she spread her fingers apart, making my knees buckle. "You need to feed," she insisted.

I'd always told her that my own arousal wasn't enough, that I needed to give her pleasure. Had she been a man, that would have been true, to an extent. But the truth was that I felt guilty, and giving Sarah orgasm after orgasm was my way of making it up to her.

She took my hand and guided me over soft flesh. When my fingers rolled across her hard nub, she gasped and I took over, rolling in soft circles and pressing her against the tiled wall.

I took her breast in my mouth, syncing the rolling of my tongue with the swirl of my fingers, bringing a sweet musk of Sarah's magic and arousal into the steaming air. When the doorbell rang, I ignored it, accepting that we'd both be going hungry tonight, but comforted by the soft moans of Sarah coming to climax because of my touch. Not my magic, not because of what I was, but because she wanted me for *me*. It was almost worth starving for.

*S*ex with my muse was always dynamic, even without the curling warmth of feeding on sexual life-force. But this time I was weak, and even though we'd brought each other to climax more than once, I lay awake and hungry as she slept curled up next to me with sheets wrapped around her like gift paper. Not to mention the rune across my stomach burned with renewed fever and the skin was starting to peel. It hissed a need inside of me that I was missing something important and it was time I stopped ignoring it.

I didn't want to deal with my nightmares right now and I laced my fingers behind my head and sank deeper into the pillow. Sarah's soft sounds as she slept next to me gave me a mixture of comfort and guilt.

I'd spoken the truth when I told her that I'd rather die than cheat on her with a man, even if I needed to feed. The last time Sarah had caught me with a guy she'd disappeared for two years. It didn't matter if she knew what I needed, it still hurt her. That heartache had been a dagger that dug a little deeper every time I came home and found our apartment empty.

Then, one day, Sarah was there, and I'd made a promise not to have sex with another guy. I'd thought that I could feed off of her, for a little while. Since she was a muse, there was a magic to her that I could taste. But it took a dangerous night where I'd almost died to realize that her magic wasn't something I could live off of. I'd been two blocks from the Succubi Den and that's when one of the regulars had found me and paid for me to have a night with their most powerful Incubi. Even then, I hadn't let him take off my clothes, but I'd fed off his kiss and the pressure of his skin against mine. It was just enough to keep me alive.

Now that I was starting to black out again, I had a decision to make. Either I was going to cheat on Sarah... or I was going to die.

$\mathcal{I}$ forced myself into a fitful sleep hoping I could run away from my problems by getting some rest. That's not how it worked and I knew that, but I was good at denial.

My standard nightmare of the end of the world raking death across the horizon took a back seat and something else took its place. There's only one thing worse than a nightmare... and that's a memory of my mother's death.

It was the last memory of my mother I only seemed to be able to recall in my dreams. She was speaking to a tattooed woman who I could only remember as a shadow. The tattoos wound around her with black wisps, blocking out her face. It was magic that I remembered and that kept drawing me back to this place. Magic that didn't want me to recall what had been done to me. Magic that had come from a witch.

My mother clutched at me as if the woman might take me away. "No!" she shouted.

The sharp tone of her voice brought tears to my eyes. She'd never told me what would happen when I turned sixteen.

"Who is this, Mama?" I asked.

The witch's voice never did come through quite right in my dream-memory. The words came out as broken, garbled sounds, like pieces of glass falling down a metal tube. "You made a deal," she hissed and reached for me.

That's right. I always seemed to forget this part when I woke up. My mother had sold her firstborn child in exchange for power over a Blood Stone... over the force of hell itself. Anger burned in me that she'd have been capable of such a thing, but the way that she bravely stepped between the witch and me said how much she regretted such a bargain and she was going to fight to have it undone.

Perhaps she imagined she'd never get pregnant. Perhaps I was a mistake and I was never supposed to have born. Regardless of her intentions, here I was, payment due, and the Witch of Shadows had come to collect her debt.

"I curse you, witch," my mother spat, even as the witch's magic ripped her out of the way.

I screamed as an invisible force dragged me to the witch's feet. Even in my dream-memory, I couldn't make out her features. Tattoos and shadows spiraled around her, but the magic couldn't wipe out the scent that filled my nostrils. Sulfur. The stench of hell wrapped around me and made me gag. This was a Witch of the Shadow Coven, one of the dark arts and old ways. Blood magic was the darkest of them all and even though I knew what was coming, I was horrified when its burning magic tingled through my veins.

I turned to look at my mother, my vision blurred as tears welled in my eyes. I hated this part, not because of the pain that came next, but because I would have loved to have seen my mother again. Even through the splotchy limit of my sight I knew she would be stunning. Sharp, angled cheekbones set on a stern face, currently tilted up in determination to use the power the witches had awarded her against them.

There was only one thing a Witch of the Shadow Coven could want with a virgin—a succubus virgin, no less.

Sacrifice to redeem a sin.

I was to resolve one of the cardinal sins. Each supernatural was capable of this twisted purpose. I sensed the sins the witch had already quelled. Four. Four sins were missing from her rotten soul.

Greed.

Envy.

Gluttony.

Anger.

That left three left to be resolved. Sloth. Pride. Lust... I knew which one I was for.

The witch raised her ceremonial dagger and moonlight glittered on its dangerous edge. I opened my mouth to scream, but no sound came out.

"You will redeem me," the witch said as shadows writhed over her face, forming a malicious grin.

I was the innocent daughter of a succubus. I could redeem a witch's sin—lust, in particular.

Witches who dabbled in dark arts eventually went to hell. There was a loophole, however. Sacrifice could get them off the hook, but not just any sacrifice. The seven cardinal sins had to be redeemed.

I buckled over when a sharp warmth spread through my belly just before the witch struck. Her blade bounced off an invisible wall with a loud *clang* that echoed through my chest and made my teeth clack.

Her eyes went wide as my mother chanted. She was the one who'd given a succubus magic, and now she dared to use it against her. My mother stretched out her hands and her mouth moved as she spoke words I didn't understand. Power hummed in the air and her necklace gleamed with ruby malice.

Her eyes found me, just for a moment, and my vision cleared just long enough to see the panic and dread that would crush my heart to pieces so badly that I'd only ever remember this moment in the depths of my worst nightmares.

"Take the power," my mother insisted as she crumpled to her knees. My mother snapped her fingers and the witch screamed, but I didn't dare turn around. I kept my gaze pinned on my mother who wove her own magic through the air. I'd never seen her do that before and I traced the gleaming red lines as they spidered and flicked the expanse between us before finally reaching my feet.

The process was slow, as was the pain. It started as a twinge deep in my belly, then a throb, and then it twisted and I whirled to find the witch contorted with it. Her shadows writhed around her as if enraged as my mother's ruby magic ripped at her.

Each sin she'd appeased filtered through the air.

The golden scale of a dragon's greed pierced the spot just above my navel and struck like the bite of a tiny but vicious insect. I cried out, but the magic held me tight as it continued its work.

The second sin came next, envy, a green and twisted rune that screwed into my skin to the right of my navel. My mother bellowed over my cries with encouragement, but I'd never been prepared for this sort of pain.

The third sin came at me, ruthless in its rage. Anger. It burned hot to the left of my navel.

I didn't have time to rest as the fourth sin, gluttony, oozed low on my stomach, dark and swollen red with blood that a vampire could gorge on for days.

Black dots sprinkled my vision. Those were the sins the witch had managed to redeem, and so those were my only guaranteed gifts. One day, I would find mates that matched those sins. The strongest of their race that would help me get revenge on the Shadow Coven for what they did to my kind, for what they had forced my mother to do to me.

The final three sins marked my body and I slumped to the ground as the world around me leapt into flames. Four sins with forgiveness, three unresolved. It would have to be enough. I would have to find a way for it to be enough.

As my dream ended, the world around me burned, and my mother took the witch with her to hell.

*T*he memories faded of a nightmare that burned hot and made my runes itch all at once. I hated that I couldn't remember it. It was as if my mind rejected any attempt at recalling the vile dream no matter how hard I tried.

It didn't matter. I was awake and I certainly wasn't getting any sleep now. Guilt stabbed harder than ever as I slunk through the midnight streets. Once again, I was drawn back to the one place that could give me some sense of reprieve.

Every step made me anxious. What if Sarah woke up and found me missing? What excuse was I going to tell her this time?

No matter how much failing Sarah terrified me, I still found myself staring at the inconspicuous Succubi Den wedged between two buildings masquerading as a massage parlor.

The round-faced succubi gave me a beaming smile as I dragged myself through the foyer. "Oh, honey, you look like you need more than a snack tonight."

I slammed all the money I had onto the counter. "Don't rub it in."

She pushed my life's savings back towards me. "He said this one would be on the house."

She dangled a familiar golden key and I

growled as shoved the money back into my pocket. I glared at her before I took her offering.

She ushered me inside and allowed me to make my own way down the hall lined with red velvet. When I unlocked the suite on the final row and swung the door open, *he* was waiting for me, and this time there weren't any sheets to obscure the view.

He leaned back against the headboard with his hands clasped behind him. His body twined with muscles and the lines at his hips pointed to a perfect cock already hard at my arrival. "I've been waiting for this," he said.

I frowned. I didn't know if it was the smug tone of his voice, or how trapped this life made me feel, but no matter how helpless I felt, there was always a choice.

With a growl I hurled the key at the ground. It clattered across marble floors as my vision wavered with red. "No," I snapped. "I'm not going to live like this."

He launched to his feet and his gaze burned with need and anger. I saw now why he'd offered a session for free. My magic had affected him just as much as he'd affected me. He needed me, wanted me for what I was. That only made me clench my jaw with determination that I wasn't going to go through with this.

"It's the rare succubus that lets herself starve." He tilted his head. "Madame said you have a girl-friend. Would she really want you to die over fidelity?"

I pinched my lips together. He was probably right. If Sarah knew I needed sex with a male to survive, she'd tell me to do it.

But her heart would be broken, and damned if I was going to be the one to break the tender heart of a muse.

"I can't do this to her," I said through clenched teeth as tears stung my eyes. "I just can't."

He crossed the room and gripped my shoulders with a strength that made my knees buckle. He pulled me close and let me rest against the hard warmth of his chest. "Madame said you're not welcome back after tonight."

I stiffened. "What?"

He tucked a strand of hair behind my ear. "This place is for those who need help. The King doesn't support what you're doing, and if word got out, the Den would be forced to shut down." He cupped my chin. "This pain you're causing yourself is pointless. After tonight, you're going to have to go back to the way it's meant to be." He leaned in and grazed his lips across my neck. "You're going to have to prey on men again and do what you do best. What you were made to do."

Pain splintered through me as I shrieked. "No!" I cried. "I won't kill to survive! I'm not a monster! Not like you."

He didn't seem hurt by my outrage. Instead he gathered the bedsheets and wrapped it around his waist. "I'm sorry. I can only hope you'll come to your senses and accept what you are, even if your *girlfriend* can't."

*A*s pissed off as that incubus made me, he'd struck a nerve. Sarah loved me, but she'd never been able to accept me for what I was. The runes across my stomach were just an oddity, not a prophecy. That wouldn't change now, not even if I ever grew the balls to tell her the truth.

I was a killer. And if I wanted to survive, I

was going to have to kill again, and the runes across my stomach were trying to tell me something important. When I looked up at the sky, those dark claws were there. I blinked twice, and then they were gone.

Perhaps it was the starvation making me see things, or perhaps it was a prophecy that I'd better start listening to.

I knew what I needed to do in order to survive. I was supposed to kill. Sarah would find out and see me for the monster than I am.

I clenched my fingers into fists and growled at the mocking sky. "I'd rather starve."

The second I arrived home, I curled into bed with a still-sleeping Sarah and let the sobs take me.

She roused from a deep sleep, her eyes still heavy with satisfaction. That only made me cry harder. "Babe," she said, wrapping her warmth and sweet magic around me, "it's okay. I'm here."

I cried into the curve of her graceful neck, and was surprised that she didn't try to pry into my head to find out what was bothering me. She was a powerful muse, capable of ripping my mind apart if she so chose.

The reality struck me like a dagger. Maybe she was afraid of what she'd find.

Forcing myself to sit up, I took her hands in mine. "Sarah?"

"Yeah?"

"Let's go to the bar tomorrow. There's something we need to talk about."

A NIGHT TO DIE FOR

Walking to the bar, Sarah noticed something was off. She wrapped her fingers through mine and gave a light squeeze. "You doing all right?"

I grit my teeth together. No, I wasn't fucking doing all right. The rune across my stomach was bleeding again, but I'd worn a bandaid this time. There was no working around what it meant. I was dying.

"I'm fine," I snapped and wrenched my hand free of hers.

She pouted before crossing the street and pushing her way into the bar. Men parted the instant she got near them, likely not even knowing that they'd been influenced by magic beyond their comprehension.

Frowning, I disapproved of how Sarah blatantly used her powers just because she was mad. I didn't want to see what she was going to do when I broke up with her in a public place, but I'd decided this would be the best way. I wanted her to think that my starvation was because I'd left her, not because I couldn't feed on her. I'd much rather her hate me... than hate herself.

"Hey!" David shouted, beaming a smile as I caught our favorite human's gaze. He waved and propped the door open. "You coming or what?"

Giving him a smirk, I waited for a motorcycle to careen by before crossing the street and brushing past David's broad chest. "Thanks for coming," I told him, honestly grateful that he'd shown.

David's beaming smile dimmed when we made our way inside and he saw that I'd brought Sarah. "Oh," he said, his disappointment obvious.

I rolled my eyes. "You're going to play the buffer, okay? We're breaking up again."

His eyes went wide, this time sparking with excitement. But he had the grace to give me a sympathetic pat on the shoulder. "Don't worry. I've got your back."

My stomach twitched, and I scratched at the rune, wondering if his touch had somehow eased the pain.

reaking up with Sarah had been one of the hardest things I'd ever done in my life. Not just because I didn't want to do it, but because my whole body screamed with agony, telling me to turn to the nearest man and take what I needed. The sheer number of penises in this place was making my jaw twitch.

The second Sarah had gotten the message that I was serious, I stormed out behind the bar, more for the relief of getting away from all the testosterone than Sarah's sad eyes. She probably thought I just wanted to get away from her, but the truth was that my world was spinning and I couldn't keep a straight face with the pain anymore. If I'd stayed in there, I'd have taken what I needed from anyone whether Sarah was watching or not.

My watch buzzed and told me I had ten minutes left to live. I turned my wrist to glance at it. Yep. This sucked.

The dark alley was hardly my first choice of where I'd die. I'd always imagined I'd go in blood-red velvet sheets stabbed with a knife from a victim who'd finally overcome my compulsion. I'd always hated what I was. This wasn't life.

Stretching out on the pebbled asphalt, I found my only bedmates were twittering mice and three empty beer cans.

I stared at the moon and contemplated if I should be doing something monumental with my last minutes. Sarah would still be inside the bar, probably wondering where I was. I could see her now, twirling a straw in a strawberry daiquiri with a pouty lip and adorable scowl. We'd broken up what, five times now? Did she even believe I was serious this time? I'd meant it. I was going to leave her for good. Not because I wanted to, but because she deserved better than me. And I deserved what would happen to me when I didn't screw men to death, literally.

And David would be next to her, telling her I wasn't worth it. Even though I knew how he felt about me, he wouldn't let Sarah think she deserved a broken heart. That's just the kind of guy he was. I'd invited him to be the buffer, but also to keep her occupied long enough to let me die in peace.

As if on cue, the wooden door creaked open and I rolled my head across the pavement to see if my angel of death had arrived.

"What'cha doin' down there, gorgeous?" David gave me a winning smile and he seemed like an angel for sure. The moonlight was drawn to him and illuminated the dark locks framing his face. The runes across my stomach twinged with pain as if recognizing him as something I needed. Perhaps it was a sin to take what I needed from him, but all sins could be forgiven, couldn't they?

I tore my gaze away. Those had been my mother's words. *All sins could be forgiven.* Had that been a lie just to try and make me feel better about myself? "What am I doing?" I muttered, trying to focus on the present before my memories ruined my last minutes alive. "Waiting to die."

He laughed and skipped down the three short

steps to the street, oblivious to my torment. "Aren't we all?"

My heart skipped when he slid down beside me, not seeming to care that we were lying on a grimy street behind an even grimier bar.

I blinked a few times before thinking of what my monumental last words should be. The world was already warping and turning grey. It was difficult to breathe and I scratched my nails across the ground, barely able to feel the pain. I'd hoped there would be a near-death experience, or something astounding to give me some miraculous insight of the world before I died. But all I could think of was the innocent girlfriend I was about to leave behind. "Do you think Sarah will be okay?"

"Sarah…" He said her name with a curl to his lip in distinct distaste. "I know you care about her, but it feels like there's something more ahead for you." He propped up on his elbow. "Have you ever considered that your feelings for Sarah are misplaced? I mean, there's something different about her that anyone would be attracted to, but you two have never been that compatible."

My eyes went wide. The runes across my

stomach all twitched in agreement, as if I'd been using Sarah as a crutch to avoid facing a future that terrified me. "What makes you say that?"

"It just, it seems right, for some reason." He sat up and pulled me with him. His strong fingers wrapping around my arm made me want to forget what I'd resolved to do. I forced myself to bring up every victim's face in my mind. Terrifying memories were always stronger than the good ones. I could still see each pale face staring back into mine, that blank look of poisoned desire masking the horror of their own death.

He tucked a lock of hair behind my ear and pulled my chin to look at him. "Are you crying?"

His blue eyes locked onto mine and I gulped down my pride. "Yes," I whispered.

His fingers trailed down my neck, extracting a sliver of my magic that wanted to wrap around his cock and lure him into giving me what I needed. He shivered as if I'd stroked him.

I squeezed my eyes shut and wished it would all be over. My watch buzzed again. I had one minute left.

His breath puffed on my lips. I couldn't open my eyes. I couldn't let him fall under my spell.

David deserved better than my sins. He was kind, sweet, and had been the only human not to immediately throw himself at me. I didn't know what had made him change his mind, but I was close to taking him up on his offer. A succubus only has so much willpower.

"Sonya..." he whispered. His voice dripped with longing and desperation.

My eyes shot open and I had nowhere to look but his concerned and adoring gaze. My tongue shot across my dry lips and hesitation tugged at my heart.

He leaned in, and fuck, I didn't pull away. I couldn't.

His lips met mine and pure ecstasy shot through my limbs. His kiss made me feel whole and I only wanted more. Any reservations I had for propriety or phantom loyalty were overwhelmed by the magic that demanded my survival. The ache deep in my bones finally sighed in relief from the sexual nourishment that flooded my senses. As if I had been wandering a desert and found a drop of life, I thrust my hands under his shirt and dug my nails across his skin and drank it all in.

How I wished I could just be human and feel

the magnetizing pull of sex without the need to feed. Then again, if I was human, I wouldn't be slipping my tongue over David's. I'd be with Sarah, happy and oblivious to what it felt like to be on the brink of death when I didn't feed.

When David's stiff arousal grated against my hips through our jeans, it was impossible not to drink his lust. I didn't have to open my eyes to know my nails were going from corpse-blue to radiant-pink. Knowing that David was literally giving me life itself only made me want him more. This was the part I couldn't fight. This was when my instincts as a predator took over.

He must have felt the drain, for his breath hitched and his eyes went wide. He stared at me, his lust clouding over with confusion. My powers kicked in out of reflex, wafting an invisible scent that made him smile as if he'd forgotten what made him startle and he groaned with pleasure, no longer able to feel the pain I was causing him. I wished I knew how my powers worked. How could something that made him look at me like that eventually kill him?

He licked his lips as if he could taste the poisonous nectar and growled as he ripped off my thin sweater, nearly tearing it in half. He didn't even notice the bandaid still plastered over the top rune that had finally staunched its throbbing ache, as if satisfied with the sexual nourishment running freely in my veins. I couldn't help but feel the rush too, some unexplainable need to have him even here, on this grimy street, even now, when Sarah could walk outside and find us together.

My heart raced as I clawed at his zipper. It didn't matter how many times I'd had magical sex. I was the most clumsy, uncoordinated creature to exist. He huffed a short laugh as he popped off the button on his jeans and slipped down the zipper with ease and his erection escaped from the confines. It was bigger than I'd imagined, and my desperate hunger paused to admire his pulsing cock.

"Like what you see?" he asked. He didn't look me in the eyes, but cupped a hand around my breast and squeezed, his face lighting up with a smile.

"Yes, I like what I see, and yes, they're real," I said with a laugh.

"I knew it!" he exclaimed. Then we laughed together, half-crazed with the disbelief of touching each other's bare skin.

Humored by the moment, and the draft of nourishment I'd already absorbed, I wiggled out of my jeans while he groped and kissed my breasts. I tucked the fabric underneath my bare ass and hoped he'd be gentle so the knobby ground didn't tear through the clothes and into my skin.

David pushed my legs apart and tested my neck with his teeth. He didn't wait for my permission and rammed into me. The thrust made me cry out with pleasure. His flesh wasn't the only thing that entered my body. The magic of his desire came in too. The two pleasures battled with one another until they combined, bringing me to climax and blossoming me back to the fullness of life.

I'd had sex with a lot of men, but making love with David behind that bar will always have a special place in my heart. Sex was always magical for me, as was my nature, but I'd denied myself for so long. On top of that, David had resisted me until my need couldn't be denied. It was as if some outward force had sent him to me, making sure that he was there when I'd been too stubborn to take what I needed to survive. To finally have him after all this time was a guilty pleasure. Like with any sin, once it was over, guilt was all that remained.

I could sense David's life dwindling. His skin had greyed just a shade paler than the moonlight should have made it seem, and there could be no doubt the deterioration had already begun.

Yet, he couldn't sense his own life leaving him. His blue eyes remained sharp and pure, as if they held his very soul and would never let go.

I wished that were true.

I shifted my gaze away and lingered on the gold chain dangling from his neck—the only article of clothing that still remained.

I slipped out from under him, grimacing as the protruding rocks speared through our pile of clothes we'd used as bedding. David had not been gentle whatsoever and my backside and shoulder blades burned with tiny cuts. I ran a finger over the rune that had lost its bandaid, but it was smooth as if soothed by the romp. I looked down at it, and even though it was still angry, it had definitely calmed. Then a voice filtered into my mind. *He's not one of the seven, but now you will survive. Find them, Sonya, find the other pieces of your heart that your mother scattered into the world. Reunite with them and fulfill your destiny.*

I froze, staring at the rune that had just fucking spoken to me. Okay, now I was really losing it.

"That was..." David said, his words drifting off with a sense of wonder. He clearly hadn't heard the voice, meaning that I was definitely losing my shit.

Trying to calm the shakes that rippled over my fingers, I focused on my watch. It'd been buzzing for the better part of thirty minutes and it was time to reset it to 730 hours—one month until I had to take what I needed again.

"That was wrong," I finished for him. David wasn't who I needed, but the prophecy had just revealed itself a little bit more to me. There were men out there who could survive sex with me, and I could survive with them. I just needed to find them.

He snapped his gaze up and I ignored him, pulling on my jeans and fighting with the button that seemed too big for the loophole.

"Wrong? That was amazing."

I tugged at the button and the wretched thing wouldn't go through. I jerked left and the threading caught my nail, tearing it the wrong way. "Damn it!"

David scrambled to his feet and stepped through one leg hole of his jeans. "Is it Sarah? After all those things you said to her—what she said to you. It's over for good, right?" He turned somber. "I've seen you two breakup before. This time seemed different. It seemed real. That's why I..." He features took on an aura of pain as he stared at me. I knew he was waiting for me to tell him he was right. But I'd meant to die. He'd given me a second chance and I didn't know what to do with it.

Not meeting his gaze, I searched the ground for my bra. A cool breeze drifted through the alley, bringing with it a sense of relief under my sweat-dampened hairline and the faint smell of garbage.

I'd get the button-hole later. At the very least, I could cover my breasts. I looked down at them and sighed at the lasting red marks of David's teeth.

The bar's door creaked open and I threw my

arms over my chest. Not that I'd expected privacy in a bar's back alley, I just didn't want to entice any further victims.

"Sonya? You out here? I—" Sarah sounded as if she was about to make an apology until she scanned the scene and drew in a deep breath as if to scream.

I threw my hands out, waving in defense of whatever accusations she was about to throw my way. Not that I had any sort of defense prepared, I just couldn't fathom Sarah being witness to my crime.

David shoved his other leg through his jeans and battled with the zipper. "Sarah, it's not what you think."

Her mouth bobbed open and closed like a fish stuck on dry land. Her pink skirt flirted with the wind, flapping around her thighs until she pushed her white hand-purse over it. Her gaze fell to her feet and she shifted, looking unbalanced on her ivory platform heels.

Then I saw what she was staring at. A black laced bra.

"God sakes." I scrambled to the steps and snatched it up, wrapping it around my chest and pulling the straps over my shoulders.

"I'm sorry, David," Sarah whispered. "You don't deserve to die."

I staggered. How dare she frighten him? Never mind if it was the truth. He still had months, if not years. I hadn't taken more than I needed...right?

She clenched her purse, as if debating to say something else before shaking her head and scampering back into the bar.

David rubbed his neck and gave a nervous laugh. "Uh, did I hear her right?"

I stiffened and bore my gaze through the closed door as if I could will Sarah to come back. Not that my powers worked that way—at least, not on women.

A cold hand on my shoulder made me jolt. "Cripes, David."

He chuckled. "Cripes? Does sex transform you into a British chick?" He smirked. "I could dig that."

"Look, I need to go after her, all right?"

His face fell. "What? Why?"

"She thinks..."

He rose one eyebrow. "That you're going to kill me?"

I scoffed and jerked away from his touch. He

couldn't find out. Not so soon. Not like this in a back alley of a bar with mice, and empty beer cans, and—where was that god awful smell coming from?

A tiny flash of light caught my eye. If I'd been angled the other way, I would have missed it entirely.

I froze. *No, it can't be...*

Another flash of light and an unmistakable, audible, *click*.

"What is it?" David asked.

I pushed him and hoped he didn't notice how my legs wobbled. "You're stepping on my sweater."

He murmured an apology as I tugged the dirtied blouse over my head.

David's skin still left its scent on mine, and somehow, someway, Mr. Anderson had caught me in the act.

JUDGMENT

I'm not one for indecision, but the overwhelming desire to make David *mine* battled with the hope that Mr. Anderson could actually save him. I'd been given a second chance at life, and David deserved one too.

The breeze drifted a can across the alley and I knew Mr. Anderson was waiting for me to make my move. If the rancid smell was any indicator, he'd probably been hiding in a dumpster. He'd definitely watched too many bad detective movies...

With one last defiant glare into the dark alley, I hopped the three steps back to the bar and ripped open the door.

"Stay with me," David pleaded. My skin

tingled with the desire to make him surrender completely. It'd only take...

I glared at him over my shoulder, feigning disgust. "I didn't mean for this to happen. Let's pretend it didn't happen and you let me go after my girlfriend." Even as I said the words, I knew they were empty. The rune across my stomach that she'd activated when we'd first met was now dormant. It didn't burn, it didn't sting, it didn't do anything. Whatever my prophecy needed from her, it'd already gotten it.

She's one of the seven... but she's not one of the four.

His eyes followed me with a sad puppy stare as I turned away. I escaped into the drunken laughter and droning music that pounded against my chest and hesitated once the door had closed. Searching for Sarah, I ran my thumb across the small ring around my pinkie finger before blundering through the crowd.

"Sarah!" I shouted, ignoring my reflection in the bartender's mirror that showed my hair spiked out at the ends like a crazed lunatic.

We had to get out of here. We had to get some distance from Mr. Anderson before he cornered me and slapped on those handcuffs he was so fond of. In any other case, handcuffs sounded like a good time, but not when it came to Detective Anderson. He was not only immune to my powers, but now he had his evidence. Real pictures of me leeching David's life. I might as well have thrown my hands up and said, "You got me!"

David's garbled cry cut through the closed door and I cringed. It took all my willpower not to go after him, but he was safer with Mr. Anderson, wasn't he? If the Detective had figured out how to thwart my gifts, maybe that meant there was a cure for the deterioration. Maybe David wouldn't have to die.

However, I didn't trust the bastard to help David on his own, even if he had the means. I'd need some backup to make sure he kept his priorities straight.

"Sarah!" I shouted again, this time more frantic.

A blonde head bobbed at the entrance and I launched myself, putting my palms together like I was going for a swan dive in an ocean made of unshaven men and whiskey. My nose pinched and I wondered how starving I'd been to have been attracted to anyone in this place.

Sarah's eyes locked onto mine a split second before she bolted outside. I knew that look. That's the look she had the last time I'd failed her. The last time someone had to die.

And she'd disappeared for two years.

I shoved my way to the front and ignored elbows stabbing my ribs. I didn't have two years this time. Mr. Anderson was right outside and he had David. I needed someone to watch him. Someone to guide him in the right direction without them knowing they were being influenced. Someone with skills I didn't have.

By the time I made it out onto the dusty street, Sarah was gone.

I was on my own.

*D*isbelief rooted me to the spot. How could Sarah abandon me? Not now, not when I needed her most.

"Move, wench!" A drunken man shoved me from behind and I stumbled.

I turned and glared at him. When his eyes met mine he locked into my spell. I slipped into my magic so easily. I couldn't resist. I'd just fed and the sexual energy made me giddy and spontaneous.

He stiffened and wavered as the wall of desire hit him. His eyes grew wide so that they looked like yellow orbs protruding from his leathery face. His tongue flicked across his dry, cracked lips.

Taking one empowering step towards him, the man faltered back with one hand pushed out in defense. A gold ring glinted against the bar's neon light.

I shoved an accusatory finger in his face. "You're going to go back home, tell your wife you're sorry, and not touch a drink again for the rest of your life. Got it?"

He swayed side-to-side, fighting against my compulsion.

I smiled sweetly, leaning in and grazing my nail across his cheek. "You understand?"

Skin contact made it solid. His shock melted into a goofy grin. "Yes, but me wife's dead."

"Do you have anyone at home?"

He pondered for a moment. "No, but me boy's struggling down in Texas. He's the only family I gots left."

"Why's he in Texas?"

He grinned as his eyes searched my face. "You're so beautiful."

"Answer me."

He blinked as if he couldn't focus. Alcohol always messed with the interrogation side of my powers. Something to do with the brain synapses not being able to connect fast enough. At least, that's what my mom had told me.

"Drinking," he answered after a moment. "I can't keep a steady job 'cuz me drinking. I drink away any money he sends me. Texas is far enough he don' have to see it. But he sends me money anyway." His gaze grew distant. "Maybe he hopes I'll use it to visit him someday."

I pressed both hands against his cheeks and resisted a gag against the sour plume of alcohol. "Then get home. Rest. And go to your boy tomorrow. Work hard and don't touch the drink again. Pay him back and earn his respect. Got it?"

He nodded against my grasp. I released him and he stumbled down the street mumbling, "Me boy, me boy."

I took in a deep breath. That inner voice tried to justify what I was. *See? You do good with your gifts. You may take a life, but how many do you save? Imagine what you could do with your four...*

I stomped my foot. It wasn't a matter of mathematics. I couldn't just justify infidelity, rape, murder...no matter how much good I did. And four? What was this damned four my nutty voice kept going on about?

I scanned the street. Parked cars judged me with their frowning grills and broken headlights. Even a few toothless hookers added their own oppressive stare for good measure.

Refocusing, I pushed away the judgment, self-hatred, and regret. That wasn't going to help David.

I wavered on my feet as I considered my options. If I couldn't find Sarah, I needed the next best thing. Maxine.

Stomping down the street with clenched fists didn't stop the fluttering in my chest. Maxine wouldn't appreciate a visit from a succubus, especially one being tracked by a detective. But I didn't have a choice. I needed help. Even if that meant getting help from a nun.

THIRD SIN'S A CHARM

My vision blurred as the sidewalk faded in and out of sharpness. Spaced-out street lights left long lengths of darkness for me to slink through like a thief in the night. Budget wasn't an issue. Seattle had more than its share of city money. Unfortunately, the crime-ridden south side of Seattle, dubbed "White Center," was known more for its bars, porn shops, and crime... None of those things enjoyed being in the spotlight.

I wrinkled my nose at a leering pair of men with hairy arms hanging out of their car window like they owned the place.

I didn't have time for this. Sister Maxine was where I was heading, not trouble.

Their beady eyes flickered with interest and I sighed. Fine. Let them try and bother me on a night like tonight. Let's see how that worked out for them.

The clicks from my heels echoed out and preceded me down the street. I shouldn't have come down this way, but I'd been preoccupied. I'd lost my girlfriend, stupidly dumped her thinking that would finally allow me to let go and die of starvation. Dumb. My aura of temptation must have been strong, strong enough to lure David out and fuck me right there on the street. And I let him. I was a fucking monster.

"Where you off to, sweetheart?" said a burly man who slinked from the beat-up Cadillac.

His buddy with a half-showing beer belly shuffled to my side and inhaled. "Smells like dessert." He grinned, giving me a bird's eye view of his row of yellowing and cracked teeth.

Being a succubus didn't mean I was blind. The drunken old man had been spontaneous. I didn't care how ugly they were when it was spontaneous. But this? The burly man stroked his beard, and I could swear there were dried pieces of meat still stuck to it. *Gross.*

I squeezed my eyes shut and leaned, holding

my arms out and letting them drape over each hairy neck like I was hugging mangy dogs.

"Fellas," I breathed in my most seductive voice. I remembered David's lips on my neck and heat swept through my chest. I let the memory engulf me until the yearning returned. I sighed and pushed it through my palms and into the men's bodies.

To control them I needed to feed them.

I screwed one eye open and their tongues were already lolling. Their eyelids fluttered and they staggered under my slight weight. Maybe I was laying it on a bit too thick.

Then I saw the fresh bloodstains on their boots.

I stumbled back and they toppled over onto the ground, wobbling around like overthrown turtles. While they were drunk and disoriented on my power, I shifted to the car and peered in.

Two women.

Dead.

Once the bastards righted themselves, they crawled to my feet and I forced my lips into a smile, focusing on the lust I tasted on my breath. A succubus' lust for vengeful death... That was a compulsion I rarely had the chance to use.

"You know what I want?" I asked sweetly.

"A spanking?" the bearded man barked.

I huffed a laugh. "Ah, yes! What a great idea. Except..." I ran my finger across his chin and ignored the nausea rolling in my stomach. "Why don't you spank your friend? With your fist, of course. Over and over again, right in his face. Do it until he stops moving. I would *love* that."

He blinked, and there was a flicker of fight in his eyes. I pressed in closer and exhaled.

He breathed in the fine dust of my power and trembled. "And then?" he asked. There wasn't a shred of disobedience left in the man.

"And then, I want you to drag him—" I pointed to the belly-man, "to the police station. Tell them what you did. Everything...you've ever done. Would you do that for me?"

The belly-man clapped his hands together like a bumbling idiot. "What do I do?"

I swept my hand over his face and purred my next words. "You die."

*T*he thumps of fist against flesh matched the steady beat of my heart and clink of my heels as I made my way to the West Seattle Bridge.

Bam.

Bam.

Crunch.

A grin smeared across my face.

I didn't mean to enjoy it. Yet, how I loved the sound of flesh on flesh. A little voice told me just to relish my handiwork. Those two murderers deserved what was coming to them.

I turned my wrist to reset my watch timer. The purple numbers pleasantly glowed as they counted down in a rush. I didn't mind taking off three hours for this. One hour per man I'd fed enough sexual energy to overcome their will. Two murderers and one dead-beat dad dealt with. Worth it.

The thought of Sister Maxine's judgmental frown splattered across my vision.

One violent shake of my head and my thoughts flung her out as quickly as they'd materialized. No sense getting myself riled up. There was only one thing I needed from Sister Maxine, and then she'd never see me again.

Cars rushed on the wet pavement as I crossed the lower street to the better part of town. This side had lights all over the place and I squinted—no, not lights. The sun was rising.

An orange glow bled above that cathedral's pike and I hurried my gait. The morning's heat and nighttime's events had made me work up a sweat and I looked forward to the cool air of the cathedral. Whoever came up with that phrase "sweating like a whore in church" clearly didn't realize they had the best air-conditioning in Seattle and the most expensive insulation to keep it in. None of that cheap crap for God.

Even if I was enthusiastic to escape the heat, I couldn't help but slow to a saunter as my gaze was drawn to the bursts of broken reds in the stained glass. I desperately tried not to think of belly-man's face.

Calling upon my skills of suppressing emotion, which were probably extremely unhealthy, I shoved the discomfort deep into my chest and assured myself that I'd feel better once I was inside. My mother had said it was the only place you could truly come to an understanding with sin, and one day, I'd have to face mine if I wanted to survive, all seven of them. I'd never paid much attention to her back then, but as I absently rubbed the runes through my shirt, I wondered if she'd been more literal than I'd realized.

My free hand's thumb twirled the small ring on my finger, reminding me my mother was gone, and all I had left of her was this silver band, along with an abandoned mansion I refused to recognize, and far too much pornography she'd promised was just for research.

The church's shadow was already cooler than the humid air drifting in the street. I gratefully took shelter and breathed out a sigh of anticipation. How would Maxine react to seeing me again after all these years?

The massive oak door rimmed with engravings was already cracked open and I slipped inside, expecting to hear the rhythmic chanting of the nuns or a boys' choir practicing their song. Instead, I heard Zack yelling at the top of his lungs.

"Sonya's out there right now fuc—" He cleared his throat, remembering he was talking to a nun. "Sonya's *killing* people! Are you going to let one teensy tiny itty bitty technicality get in the way?"

Sister Maxine's unmistakable no-nonsense voice boomed through the foyer. "Technicality?" she screeched. "That's hardly a *technicality.*"

Tugging off my shoes, I shifted against the wall and peered around the corner.

Zack crossed his arms and stared down his nose at Sister Maxine with smoky eyes. I swear, I wish he'd stop using eyeliner. Though... it did kind of make him look sexy. Like some sort of exotic rock star.

"Sonya can't just go around killing people. When she was finding douchebags to feed off of, that was one thing. At least she was subtle. But now she's after random blokes behind a bar? No. This is the only solution."

Sister Maxine thumped her rosary beads against his chest. "Does the Lord's word mean nothing to you?"

I balked. Don't tell me he came here to...

Zack weighed both hands down on Maxine's tiny frame. "If it held any weight in my heart, do you think my first girlfriend would still be alive?"

I buried my face in my hands. Fornication. He

was talking about fornication, and more impor-
tantly, the first fornication I'd ever had. Sure,
great conversation with a Nun.

THE FIRST OF FOUR

Luke

So many sounds escaped my body that made me feel like some kind of beaten animal. I couldn't help it. The pain tore out of me and became a creature of its own.

"Shut it, freak! Or I'll come down there and knock your teeth out!" Detective Anderson yelled down the dank stairway.

Why couldn't he ever use my name? And it wasn't just him, it'd been the kids at school, strangers on the street, heck, even my own family members. No one ever called me Luke. Well, except my mother. Though when she called me Luke it came with my middle name "Mitchell" and a twitching left eye.

Sadly, even memories of my mother couldn't bring me out of my misery. I writhed on the grimy floor and my cheek slid against caked dirt and unpolished cement. The pain tumbled its way through my stomach and ripped out of my throat with a primal release of agony.

Detective Anderson yelled again, but I couldn't make out what he'd said this time. He was probably upstairs in the lab, either studying the blood he'd taken from me, or cleaning up the mess of it off that damned pristine floor. Not sure why he always cleaned it up if he was just going to rip me open again.

Thinking of the lab made me relive the last five hours of torture. It blurred together with my weekly episode of agony. Pain, I've discovered, is a sentient thing. It's alive, and it can take over your body in ways you'd never thought possible. Pain made me screech, or cry, or even defecate. A year of this shit has made me appreciate pain for what it is. My body was punishing me for being unable to protect myself from harm. Every nerve that lit up under my skin with a razor blade of fire was the cost of my own stupidity. I can't do anything about it now. It's just the price I have to pay.

Pinching my fingernails into my palms added an indecipherable sensation to the symphony of agony. I reminded myself I needed to save it all up. Keep all of this pain for myself, because when I finally got out of here, I was going to give it *all* back.

For now, I closed my eyes and drifted into the bittersweet relief of unconsciousness where only my nightmares could rival reality.

When I'd woken, the pain had retreated to a dull ache and I could only tell it was still there if I tried to breathe. Unfortunately, I'm no different than other humans in that I do actually need oxygen to some extent, so when I tried holding my breath and pretended everything was back to normal, reality came rampaging back with a fit of wet coughs. Twinges sparking through my chest reminded me where Anderson's knife had slid through my ribs. Each breath brought a fresh pinch biting through my skin. I shifted, trying to find a more comfortable position and my leg throbbed, still healing from the pieces of bone fusing together in my cracked leg.

This wretched body needed eight hours to heal. The level of pain told me I had two or three more hours to go.

I eased my way to the corner of my cell. Pressing against the damp cement made me feel like there was something solid to hold onto. Floating in a nightmare wasn't how I'd keep sane. A year of perpetual darkness can make a man go mad. But my mother had done this to me sometimes too, so maybe that's why I was used to it. Not the torture or anything like that, but the isolation. A man didn't need training to handle torture. People are born with a certain pain tolerance, and either they can take it or they can't. Pain is just a biological response, but being left alone with your senses deprived tricks a person into thinking they're already dead. To survive isolation isn't innate. It's trained.

Only a fortune teller could know I'd need such insane training. Unfortunately, or fortunately, depending on how you looked at it, my mother was a bonafide psychic. She'd tried to tell me that her destiny was linked to three, which meant I was next in line. There would be three others I was linked to as well, all for the purpose of the girl I had to save. I never knew what she meant by that.

Until Detective Anderson had locked me down here, I'd thought my mother a bonafide psycho as well. When I'd turned eight she'd begun my "training." She'd throw me in the basement and let me scream until I fell asleep, and wouldn't come back for me for a whole day, sometimes two.

She always cried every time she brought me back into the light. I remembered how even the soft living room lamps burned my retinas and looked like tiny suns casting beams across the room. I'd tremble and cling to her, even though she was the one who'd left me all alone. She'd just stroke my hair and tell me that I needed this, and one day I'd understand.

When I'd turned thirteen, I'd gotten enough sense to alert the authorities. Of course, she'd seen that too. And through the tears she'd told me to forgive myself for doing it to her. She'd understood, and it was a small price to pay for keeping me alive.

I clung to the hope that one day I *would* forgive myself, because ever since I realized what she'd sacrificed for me, still rotting away in a cell, forgiveness seemed impossible. The only comfort was that I was in a cell too, and could live out my term just as she was now.

She'd been right about everything. Once I'd learned the truth, I'd wracked my brain trying to think of any wisdom she'd offered from her visions through the years. Which was difficult when at the time, I'd thought everything she'd said was psychotic rubbish. All I could remember was the last vision she'd given me, and her assurances that even though I'd reach the limits of my endurance, I *would* survive. Given my manifesting powers of regeneration when I was a teen, I didn't need a psychic to tell me that.

I pressed my fingers into my eyes as I tried to recall anything useful. The motion sent pain jabbing through my cheek and eye socket as I snagged dried blood. With a short chuckle I couldn't believe I'd forgotten he'd taken the eyeball during this torture session. What did he imagine he could do with it? Was there some black market for creepy grey eyes? Sure, my eye had already grown back. My broken bones always healed, my plucked organs regenerated, but it didn't mean he'd learn anything from taking them out. My regeneration wasn't fucking *scientific*. It was supernatural, and he knew it.

After I'd peeled off the scab, I crawled and roamed my hands across the floor hoping to find a bottle of water. If it was past evening, I wouldn't always get dinner, but I'd get water. I couldn't regenerate my own fluids, and my new left eye felt like some kind of deflated leather balloon.

My fingers struck the soft plastic and the delightful *swoosh* of moving water made me crack a smile. That was the trick in isolation. Make tiny goals, and when you can accomplish one, enjoy the shit out of it.

As slow as physically possible, I relished each finger that wrapped around the bottle. The cool water stole my heat without adding more dirt to cake onto my skin, and I reminded myself to enjoy the small reprieve.

I set the bottle upright and ran my finger around the lid. It was rimmed, and the shape of it meant it was a Dasani bottle. Damned Anderson, why'd he have to buy water with sodium added? I didn't need more salt. That was for sure.

Closing my eyes, I chided myself for not fully appreciating my water. It was water...with *minerals* added. Don't think about the sodium. Appreciate what you've got, Luke.

Just as I was about to take a sip, a searing beam of light cascaded down the stairs, and my right iris desperately retracted. My left eye wasn't as functional and sent shooting pains through my skull as it absorbed every bit of luminescence before it sluggishly shrunk.

"Looks like you've got a new roommate, freak. Isn't that nice?" Anderson sneered as he dragged a body down the steps. "Been a while since you've had any company."

My vision finally adjusted and I leaned against the iron bars. Anderson let the body thump down each step while he sauntered with an unceremonious stagger.

"What's the problem, no muscle to do your dirty work?" I retorted, my voice coming out hoarse from all the screaming I'd done.

Anderson shot me a glare. "For someone in your position, your consistently cocky attitude amazes me."

I pressed my face against the bars and tried to

look bored, but in reality, the pits of my stomach were desperately trying not to retch bile.

Anderson had some unconscious guy rolling down the steps, and I pitied the poor soul when he woke up. His pale face was marred by a streak of red where he'd been struck on the temple. But I knew that color of pale. It wasn't from blood loss. His lips were white, and his cheeks were sunken in. This guy had been fed on by a fucking succubus.

FORNICATION

Sonya

"**Z**ack!" I shouted as I spun around the corner.

Both Sister Maxine and Zack turned their startled stares at me, and then their shoulders eased as if they'd been expecting my arrival.

Zack offered me a devilish grin paired with a flirtatious wink. "Since when do you attend Mass?"

My lips puckered. "Funny. Look who's talking."

We matched each other's glares until I decided I didn't want to play this stupid smoldering-gaze game. He always won, anyway.

"Did Sarah put you up to this?" I asked.

"She didn't put me up to anything. She told me about David." He rubbed his neck and his loose shirt draped, giving me a glimpse of the perfect arch across his collarbone. "After something like that, where else would you go?"

I sighed and slunk up to Maxine's side. "Long time no see, Sister."

Sister Maxine narrowed her gaze and set her bony fists on her hips. "You can't just come barging into the Lord's house justifying your sins." She thrust a pointed finger at the confessional. "You're supposed to admit all wrongdoings! Not arrogantly wave them in my face!"

I perched my hands on my hips and desperately tried to ignore Zack's crude inspection, looking me up and down and offering approving nods at my tight sweater. "Look," I said. "Just hear me out."

"Is it true? This…" She twirled her hands as if at a loss for words. "David…business?"

"Yes, yes. I slept with David."

"More fornication!" Maxine bellowed and threw her hands up in disbelief.

"Hey! I had one minute left to live. That's

sixty seconds. You can't suggest I just let myself die."

"That's your own fault," she countered. "You're more than capable of finding a husband with your looks and... skills... and not break any of the Lord's laws. Why'd you let time run out and resort to sin?"

"Seriously? You're going to sit there and turn a blind eye to seducing someone with supernatural gifts, as if it's not against any of these so-called laws."

Maxine straightened. "Who am I to question the Lord's creations? If he created you, then you have a purpose." Her eyes narrowed to slits. "But it's your responsibility to keep your abilities within the law."

Zack slipped his arm around my waist. "Don't be so hard on her. She was just trying to be loyal to Sarah. Right, love?"

Maxine buried her face in her hands. "Homosexuality? That's even worse!" She thrust her hands to her sides and balled them into fists. "Don't you think there's a reason your gifts don't work on women?"

"Sure," I bit out, the word bitter in my mouth. "Because I need a relationship where my mate doesn't *die*," I sneered and wriggled out of Zack's grasp.

"Enough bickering, ladies," Zack said. "Let's—hey, is that blood?" he asked, pointing to my jeans, then tugging at my sweater where my rune had started to bleed again.

Attention span of a moth…

I sighed. "Cripes. Whose side are you on?"

Zack chuckled. "You sound like Mom when you get all flustered." He ran a finger under my chin. "It's cute."

"Is it David's?" Maxine's quavering voice asked, her eyes glued to the bloodstains on my clothes.

I rolled my eyes. "I'm not a vampire. The blood on my boots is just from some thugs. Unfortunately, it's not their blood. They killed these girls and—"

Maxine turned green.

Zack chuckled. "C'mon. Don't get her all worked up. She *is* a nun."

"Then help me get my mom's necklace and get out of here already!"

Maxine blinked. "If you think your mother entrusted me with that necklace just so you could—"

Zack draped an arm over Maxine's shoulder. "Now, now. That's why I'm here, all right? It's either give Sonya here the necklace, or I'm going to have to get her some power another way." He leered at me. "I believe you said it broke some law in the good book? I can survive her, you know. One night with me and—"

"Yes," Maxine confirmed, cutting him off, then sighed as her arms hung in defeat. "Fine. Come with me."

Maxine shuffled away.

Before I could follow, Zack wrapped both arms around my waist and pulled me in close, pushing his lips against my ear. "Looks like you're finally getting that blasted necklace 'cuz of me." He groped his hands across my breasts and squeezed, filling me with desire mixed with mortification. I'd only slept with Zack once, and as fun as it was, he rubbed me the wrong way. His voice caressed me anyway, building a heat between my thighs. "I think I deserve a reward," he purred.

*I*f I hadn't just fed, I would have fallen lips-first into Zack's influence. I may be a succubus, but he's an incubus... and much more powerful than I at the art of seduction. When I was sixteen, I had troubles unlocking my powers and had almost starved to death. I couldn't feed on humans. I tried—my lucky prom date didn't die. Only an incubus could trigger my powers to their full potential. He'd been one of the incubi to hang out with me when I was growing up. He was my friend, not my lover, but that night, I'd needed him. Ever since then I'd craved what he had to offer. But other than unclogging the succubus plumbing, I couldn't live off him forever. Screwing him was just a quick fix. It was like swapping spit. Kind of gross and left foreign bacteria in my mouth that'd just linger for days. Does that sound disgusting? Because it is.

I threw his hands off. "Enough. I'm here for the necklace and I'm going to save David with it. I can't let Sarah think I meant for this to happen."

Zack chuckled. "If you say so. But," he thrust his finger in my face before curling it around my collar and tugging me close. "One night with me and you won't need a lay for a year." He tilted his head with amusement. "Imagine what you could do in a year not spent finding some poor sod to fuck? You could even scurry back to Sarah for a little while."

Why was he toying with me? The lust lingered in the air between us, and I knew he could taste it. That just made it even worse.

I jerked away and resumed walking towards Maxine's stiff frame. She may be old, but she wasn't deaf.

"I don't need you," I said over my shoulder. "Once I have my mother's necklace, I'll have all the power I need."

"You'll see," he called as I walked away. "You're going to need to charge that thing. Then you're going to be begging for me!"

I clenched my fists and didn't turn around, keeping my eyes fixed on Maxine's steady gait as we headed deeper into the cloister.

I was glad Zack didn't follow and the heat on my skin cooled as I focused on Maxine's bulbous black habit rolling around on her behind. What could be less sexy? Perhaps that was the point.

"Here we are," she said as we reached the end of the impossibly long hallway.

I huddled up behind her shoulder and peered at the ancient door. It felt like I was in some Merlin movie and was about to gain entrance to the hidden treasure everyone was trying to get. The door even had handsome engravings of runes in the wood that made it seem mystical and surreal.

Maxine pulled a rusted key from her pocket and fiddled with the lock. The mechanism gave a reluctant *click* and the door creaked open.

Maxine stepped inside and flicked the light switch.

The small room didn't disappoint. Thick velvet drapes framed massive oak chests, making it look like we were inside a monastery that housed the most precious of religious artifacts. The lights glimmered with the soft glow of modest chandeliers covered with frosted glass. The way the lights flickered made them seem like candles and added to the ambiance that I'd walked into a Merlin movie.

"Where's the necklace?" I asked impatiently. Every second wasted was a second less David had to live.

"What made you change your mind?" Maxine asked, placing both hands on the smallest chest perched on the room's only table. "Your mother entrusted it to me for a reason. She said it was dangerous until you had completed the destiny you were born into."

It was strange for a Nun to prattle on about Succbi magical destinies, but she was one of our allies. She knew all about the supernatural community, and that was saying something. There were few humans who'd been accepted into the fold.

My gaze swept over the room, taking in other locked boxes that contained supernatural treasures. Holy ground was the only place we'd store any sort of relic and it took a strong woman like Maxine to guard it. I knew under the frowns and stern face, there was more than met the eye.

I frowned and resisted scratching my runes that had started to bug me again. "It's time."

"Anything in particular bring you here?" she asked, still pressing for more answers I didn't have.

I'd known about my mother's necklace, that it could give me exactly what I needed to survive. With the power of a Blood Stone, I could swear off men and be with Sarah without any problems, but there had to be a catch. The dark magic lingering inside my chest roiled just being close to it. There would be a price to pay for such a prize and I'd never been brave enough to test it.

I rotated my watch around my wrist, not looking at the timer. "Because, now it's just not about me," I admitted. "I fed on David. He's a human. If there's anything I can do to save him, then I must do it."

She offered me a sad smile and a nod. She cupped a box that hummed with familiar power and creaked the small box open, revealing the necklace my mother had always worn around her neck. The chain had always been just long enough to rest it in her cleavage; a silver locket with mesmerizing swirls encrusted along the edge.

Maxine stepped aside and I faced the powerful relic, taking one trembling hand and grazing my finger across the metal. I should have been able to feel the leftover sexual energy still trapped inside. My breath caught in my throat as I took the treasure in my hands and forced myself to pop it open.

A single red gem, a lost precious stone to the history books cradled in the locket's setting.

Some would mistake it for a ruby, but my mother had taught me what it really was. A Blood Stone.

A tear rolled down my cheek. It should have been bright red, yet the Blood Stone had lost all its color and was completely white, looking like a cloudy diamond. A human would call it a moonstone, not really knowing what it was.

The Blood Stone was empty, and if I wanted to save David, I'd need to charge it...

I'd need to fuck Zack.

SPEECHLESS

Luke

I'd grown so accustomed to silence during the spanning hours in-between Anderson's torture sessions that it was unnerving to hear my cellmate's breathing. But after a while, the sensation grew on me. The soft intake and exhale drew me in until I measured each one, marking its minute difference from the last. His breaths came in long and deep, holding for a second before releasing. He seemed so calm, and somehow it made me feel safe.

When the breathing stopped, my heart flung into my throat. I rushed to the bars and beat my palms against the slick iron. "Hey. You okay, dude?"

His sharp intake of breath followed by a ragged cough sent relief flooding into my chest. It was just human sleep apnea.

My panic had woken the poor guy from his slumber. He groaned and scuffled across the ground. It was pitch black and if I were him, I'd be freaking out right about now.

"Hey. It's all right. Over here," I offered.

An incoherent grumble preceded dragging steps towards my location. Finally, a warm hand fumbled against mine. I stiffened, not used to physical contact that wasn't followed by blinding pain. But I kept my hand where it was. For once, someone needed me. Someone innocent who didn't deserve to be here. The least I could do was offer comfort.

His hand slid around mine, as if there would be Braille on my skin to explain where the heck we were. "Who's there?" he asked.

I plastered a smile on my face and even though he couldn't see it, perhaps the gesture would seep through my words. "My name's Luke. I'm a prisoner here, just like you."

The grip tightened around my fingers. "Prisoner?"

"Yeah." I shifted uncomfortably, my hand growing sweaty under his clammy touch. Damn, the guy's skin was freezing. "What's the last thing you remember?" I asked.

A moment of silence. Then he said, "I'd finally got my shot with Sonya. But then it all went wrong, and some bum must have attacked me from behind. I don't know how I got here."

I finally couldn't take it anymore and withdrew from the bars. "Sonya? Is that the succubus?"

A short chuckle. "What makes you call her that? Though she is damn irresistible. I know I couldn't keep my hands off her."

Shit. I'd hoped he'd been simply fed on, maybe she got in a lick or two. But if he'd gone all the way, he was a dead man walking. I tried to keep the panic out of my voice. "Did you fuck her?"

"Excuse me? What kind of question is that?"

I crossed my arms, now getting annoyed. "You're in a pitch-black cell, talking to a fellow prisoner, and you find my *question* odd?"

As if it hit him this wasn't a dream, he rushed

to the bars. The sound of metallic jewelry clanking against the metal made my ears hurt. "Where the fuck am I? Who are you?"

"I already told you, I'm a prisoner, just like you. If you slept with this Sonya girl, and she's a succubus, then that's why you're here. Anderson must think he can learn something from you, or use you to get to her somehow." I shifted my weight and grunted. "He's obsessed with supernaturals."

A moment of silence, then he asked, "What are you?"

"Ah," I said, spearing my finger up in the darkness, "now you're asking the right question. Too bad even I don't know what I am. I just know what I'm not, and that's human."

A sea of fluorescent lights blinked across the ceiling. Out of reflex, I snapped my eyes shut. But I'd still been too slow. Black dots sprinkled my vision when I tested my sight again, revealing the abhorrent contents of my cell. Anderson hosed it down once in a while, but man, I was starting to feel like a cat stuck in a litter box that never got emptied. Except I had way more than nine lives, which Anderson loved to remind me.

I tensed, expecting to see Anderson and his

tools of torture. He favored the good ol' hammer and nails, but to extract my eye he'd used only a spoon. When I got out of this place, I'd never be able to have tea again.

When my vision cooperated and revealed a petite blonde instead, I blinked in confusion. I was about to say, "My, Mr. Anderson. You've changed," which I found quite witty and chuckled to myself, but when I opened my mouth to impress the pretty lady with my mad joke skills, complete gibberish came out instead.

I coughed, rubbed my face, and tried again. "Blurg mangaravatah!"

She blinked and tilted her head. "Uhm, excuse me?"

What the hell was that? I'd heard of an attractive woman rendering a man dumb, but this was ridiculous.

My cellmate pressed his face against the bars. "Sarah! What're you doing here?"

Relief flooded her face. "David!"

I passed my gaze between the pair. "Humaga?" I blurted, which was my attempt at asking if they knew one another.

They both turned to consider me. "He was speaking fine a minute ago. Maybe he's been locked up too long." David shivered. "What the hell is this place?"

After taking a glance at my cell, Sarah seemed to have dismissed me as unimportant and focused on David. "So, are you hurt?"

David rubbed the back of his head. "I got a nasty hit by some bum or something, and woke up in a fucking cell. I wouldn't say my day's going so great."

Sarah backed away and hovered her fingers over the light switch. David's eyes widened. "Hey, what're you doing?" He rushed to the bars again. "Look, I know you and Sonya had just broken up and I'm sorry to make a move so fast. But you should have seen her. She was devastated. She *needed* me."

Sarah scoffed. "You're right. She did need you. But you have no idea what for."

The lights clicked off.

$10,000 WHISKEY

Sonya

I snapped the locket closed and headed for the door.

"Where are you going?" Maxine asked.

I paused at the doorway, leaning on the frame to prevent myself from falling over.

"I'm sorry." It was all I could say before breaking into a sprint and leaving Maxine behind.

I couldn't get out of this place fast enough. The clicks of my heels beat against the walls as if the very sound waves wanted to escape. Each corridor led to the next and I started to worry I couldn't remember the way out on my own.

I practically grew up in this damn place. Could I really not remember how to get out?

Finally, I made it to the dimly lit foyer and burst through the doors in a whirlwind of exasperation and relief.

Zack was waiting on the stoop staring at his phone and I tugged his shoulder after catching my breath. "C'mon. Let's go."

He huffed a short laugh and draped his arm around my shoulder as we walked away from the cathedral. "So, is the necklace empty?"

I nodded.

He sighed. "Look. I didn't want to be right."

"Yes, you did," I snapped. He'd been trying to get back into my pants ever since prom.

He chuckled and motioned me to follow him down the street. "You're going the wrong way."

"Huh? But my place is that way."

He shook his head. "We're not going to your place," he said before stuffing his hands in his pockets and following the sidewalk.

I'd never seen Zack like this before. His shoulders drooped and he kept his eyes cast down at his feet. Even his usual cocky "I know I'm hot" strut had transformed into a solemn shuffle down the sidewalk.

"So," I ventured, "if we're not going to my place, which has unlimited Oreos and beer, by the way, where are you taking me?"

He chuckled. "I don't know if it beats that but," he patted his back pocket, "I texted Derek while you were with Maxine. Luckily, he's in town."

I balked. "*The* Derek? Since when do you *text* with the oldest incubus on the planet?"

"Since he found out that you had a Blood Stone."

I clutched the necklace now hanging around my neck. It was cold and lifeless. "Well, he's not getting his mitts on it."

"Relax. It's not like that."

"Then what's it like?"

He swerved and glared down at me. "Trust me this once, will you?" He grasped my necklace, pulling my body close to his. "You know how I feel about you," he whispered, placing a soft kiss on my forehead and my ears went hot. "But your mom told me about your destiny long before you ever accepted it. I'm not one of your four, hell, I'm not even one of your sins." His thumb ran over the cool metal of my necklace. "I'm not capable of changing this for you, but I have a feeling I know who can."

He pressed his lips lightly against mine, briefly letting me taste the salty residue of his lust, and then spun around, stomping off down the street, leaving me gasping for breath.

I huffed and clamped my mouth shut, trailing after him and pushed down the butterflies fluttering in my stomach.

After a few moments of hearing nothing other than Zack's shuffling feet and my own clicking heels, we finally came to a halt.

"There we are," Zack said.

There was nothing other than a limo with its headlights still on.

Wait.

"Are you shitting me?"

Zack smiled and crossed the street. I tried not to let my jaw hang open as I followed him and stared at the glistening paint job before he opened the door.

We were really going to see the freaking Incubus King.

*Z*ack loved luxury, especially the overindulgent, expensive kind. His radiating smile filled me with warmth and when he opened the door and I slipped inside, I saw how indulgent the limo really was.

Sheer silk curtains draped across the tinted windows, bubbling champagne and bottles of whiskey were hooked into the upper cabinet, and a massive TV hung where a sunroof should have been.

I swallowed and settled across from two well-dressed security guards that blended in with the luxurious interior.

I'd always gone through life just as any human would, never using my ability to wrap any man around my little finger to an unfair advantage. I'd had a weak moment once or twice, but how could I be selfish? Any moment of weakness meant death. *David...*

I scooted down the long seat and Zack slipped in behind me.

"So," I asked the statuesque guards, "what're you, FBI agents or something?"

The one closest to me pulled off his glasses and leaned an elbow on his knee. His piercing blue eyes bore into mine and I wondered if he was really human. My insides lurched as our gazes met and a rune among the four blazed with heat, making me buckle over and grab it. It wasn't pain, but an intense pleasure that took me off guard.

"Better than the FBI," he said, his voice husky as if he sensed the impact his mere presence had on me. "We're the King's Guard," he replied with a sidelong smirk.

I rolled my eyes as the sensation faded. My runes were just confused. This guy was not one of the seven I was looking for.

One of the King's guard, hmm. Even if that was true, he didn't have to make it sound so ridiculous.

The human leaned back in the leather seat, spreading his legs like men tend to do when they think they have ten pound balls that can't be bothered to be grazed by their supposedly massive thighs.

Zack cleared his throat and shoved the guy down a few inches so that he could sit across from me. "Who's the incubus here? You or me?"

The guard frowned and crossed his arms. "My father's an incubus," he muttered.

Zack chuckled. "It only carries down from the female gene. Tough luck, bro."

I smiled at the guard in spite of the revelation. At least I knew where his good looks came from, and perhaps why he'd confused my prophecy. Depending on the lineage of his father, he might have some relation to the pull of the dark magic I'd been running from.

The guard winked at me and tapped the window. The limo eased into motion and pop music began to play. The TV overhead blipped on and displayed a bunch of attractive dancing girls rubbing up on each other in a club.

Zack breathed out a sigh and leaned over to run his fingers across the array of bottles. "What's your poison?"

I smiled. "Whiskey, please."

He nodded and plucked the largest bottle from the selection. The second security guard popped open a shiny black compartment, revealing dazzling crystal glasses I'd only seen in magazines.

As Zack poured me a drink, he flashed my necklace a glance, his eyes lingering there for a while.

My hand shot up to it, and I realized the

necklace was neatly tucked in my cleavage, just like it always had been with mom.

"It's bad enough you want to screw me. Don't get hot on me because I remind you of my mother," I said.

He laughed and handed me my drink. "Relax, will you? I wasn't thinking of her, and I never slept with her. Don't be gross."

I snorted a laugh. Oh, so *that* was the line he wouldn't cross.

The heavy aromas from the golden whiskey drifted up and kissed my nose. *Oh man.* I brought it to my lips and ventured a sip. My eyelashes fluttered and a moan escaped my throat as the delicious silk slid across my tongue.

Both security guards fidgeted, but Zack leaned in with a smile, his own whiskey on his breath. "So," Zack said, "you like ten thousand dollar whiskey. Why am I not surprised?"

I glared and finished off my glass, enjoying the creeping warmth that spread through my chest.

Zack offered me a refill, but I declined. No one was sexy plastered—not even me.

I leaned my head back on the cold headrest and watched the girls dance on the TV. The whiskey burning in my belly made it seem as if the cabin swirled and I was dancing with them as I rolled my head side to side with the beat.

The moment burst as Zack's phone buzzed obnoxiously against the seat, sounding like a dentist's drill searing into my brain.

I lifted my head to glare at him, but he was staring at the screen as if he wasn't sure if he should answer. Then he bit his lip—cripes that's cute—and tapped the screen before pressing it to his ear.

"Yeah. She's with me," he said and shot me a glance.

"Who is it?" I mouthed.

He shook his head and swatted me away.

"Really?" he asked the caller, his eyes going wide.

I pinched his knee and he flicked off my fingers with an agitated glare.

"Should I tell her?" he asked.

"Tell me what?" I snapped and Zack pressed the phone against his chest and shushed me.

He lifted the phone to his ear again. "Okay. No. I'll text you the address. Yeah, we'll meet up tomorrow."

He tapped the side of the phone and it offered a click. Then Zack considered his glass, took a generous sip, and slouched into his seat.

I narrowed my eyes to slits. "Who was that?"

He tossed his phone, letting it somersault before catching it in mid-air. "Sarah," he said casually.

I lurched across the short expanse of the cabin and latched onto his knees. "What'd she say? Where is she?"

He chuckled. "Wouldn't you like to know?" He swiftly spread his legs and I tumbled face-first into his groin.

I lurched back with a snarl as he bellowed with laughter and sloshed his whiskey. "Aw, don't make me spill this liquid gold, girl. If you wanted a taste all you had to do was ask." He offered me a sly grin and even the security guards smothered their laughter.

"This isn't a game," I snapped and glared at all of them.

Zack wiped the tears from his eyes. "Relax, all right? Sarah is working her magic until you can get the Blood Stone."

I crossed my arms and slumped. "If Anderson can resist me, what makes her think he won't resist her?"

Zack shrugged. "Your powers aren't always reliable." A mischievous glint sparked in his eye. "Perhaps I need to help sort you out again."

Ignoring the tempting invitation, I rolled the empty glass across my palms. "I already have the Blood Stone," I said, changing the subject. "You didn't tell her it needs to be charged?"

"Hell no. She'd just run off and leave David to die rather than let you charge that thing on your own."

I swallowed the rising bile. "She's that against it?" I was going to have to give in and sleep with an incubus to charge it, and I guessed King Derek would know who'd be strong enough to help me. Not that I knew what he wanted in return, but one night would be worth it to help David and be with Sarah guilt-free, right?

Zack's eyes softened before he looked down at his half-emptied glass. "That's between you two."

I stuck out my lower lip in a pout and pushed myself further into the leather seat. What was Sarah thinking? The only reason I'd gotten Mom's necklace in the first place was because I'd thought she'd abandoned me. If my powers were really going wonky, I needed the boost to take on someone as dangerous as Anderson without her.

I ventured a gaze to Zack. "If Sarah is with Mr. Anderson, does that mean she thinks she can save David?"

Zack scoffed. "You know what? You and Sarah are perfect for each other. You're hopeless romantics." He clicked his tongue. "As if there's a cure for the deterioration." His eyes locked onto mine. "Don't you understand what you do when you feed? Your powers have a cost to maintain."

I frowned. "What if I don't want these stupid powers?"

He gave an exasperated sigh. "Sonya. Just accept what you are already. Get with the program and use your powers for once. You need to take out that Anderson bastard. Don't make Sarah do your dirty work."

I frowned. "Is she safe on her own? Should we send someone?"

He chuckled. "There you go, giving her too

much credit for one thing and not enough for another. She's a muse. Nobody's going to touch her if she doesn't want them to." His eyes narrowed. "You just better hope what she wants is still you. Nothing worse than a pissed off muse. That's how the Dark Ages got started."

NINE LIVES

Luke

That Sarah chick was a muse, wasn't she? There was only one supernatural in the world who can fuck with someone's brain other than a succubus, and if my mom's mad ramblings had taught me anything it was to stay the fuck away from a muse. Too bad I was in a locked cell with nowhere to go, stuck with a fucking brain-killing muse just two feet away.

"Sarah, you still there?" David's voice pierced the darkness.

The door to the security room creaked open, shedding a faint red light across the cement floor. "Will you shut up?" she hissed. "I'm trying to help you. Which is going to be tenfold more difficult if you let Anderson know I'm here."

I rubbed my temples. She wasn't going anywhere soon. That was for sure. And every second she stayed, her aura burrowed deeper into my skull like one of those brain-sucking monsters I'd seen on Saturday cartoons. Except, instead of a purple cloud with fangs teething at my brains, a gorgeous girl hid in the shadows and wouldn't... fucking... leave.

"Blargalargalarg!"

"Will you tell Luke to shut it, too?" Sarah asked.

We all fell silent when the door two floors up slammed shut. That was the lobby, and there were only two kinds of people who came into the lobby: corrupted police officials and the psycho detective.

Unfortunately for me, it was the latter.

I recognized his gait by now, the way he slunk down the steps like a drunken raccoon. The *swish, swish* of his faux silk pants made the hairs on the back of my neck stand on end. It didn't really matter if I had a day or a week to prepare myself for this moment. The promise of torture always made my knees go weak.

As I curled into a ball, the lights blinked on. Anderson pranced across the floor and seemed to enjoy the fact that his collection of prisoners had grown. "Let's see. Who gets to play first?"

David slammed against the bars. His cheeks were sunken in and his muscles trembled. The deterioration was slight, but it was there. "Who the hell are you?" David demanded. Even if his body showed all the signs, I was struck by the intensity of his ice-blue eyes and his demeanor that he'd rip Anderson apart the second he got a shot.

Anderson slunk to the cell. "Detective Anderson. Pleased to meet you." He extended his hand for a handshake, then chuckled. "Ah, right, you're my prisoner."

"And why, exactly, am I your prisoner?"

Anderson rubbed his stubbly chin and cast me a glance. He was putting on a good show, but he always shaved. Something had him rattled. "You're going to help me," Anderson growled in response to David, "just like my freak here."

David snarled. "Why would I help you? You're a fucking maniac!"

Anderson smiled. "It's cute that you think you have a choice." He reached into his coat pocket and pulled out a small gun with a plastic tip. The tranq. I hated that thing.

One silent *plup*! and David was out on the floor with a dart sticking out of his chest.

Anderson cast me a glance as he unlocked David's cell. "You're quiet. No jokes today?" He grinned. "Cat got your tongue?" He loved that joke. Cats have nine lives. Haha. Hilarious. It'd lost any humor it might have had once I'd gotten through enough mortal wounds to vastly surpass nine lifetimes.

I frowned and cast a glance to the security room where Sarah's blue eyes peered through the darkness. I flicked my gaze back to Anderson.

Anderson hesitated, and then looked to the security room.

I wasn't sure if Sarah was friend or foe. History didn't favor the muse as a species. They were just too strong, capable of burrowing into people's brains and seeing whatever they wanted to see, and making people do whatever they wanted them to do.

Though, seeing her triggered my mother's vision. At the time, I'd thought my mother had drugged me and I was having one hell of a trip.

The vision had said I would have to wait in this cell until a woman came, and only I could help her embrace the fate of four. If I didn't intervene, then supernaturals would overrun the world. And not the good kind, if there was such a thing.

But Sarah, she couldn't be the girl I was waiting for. I was waiting for someone pure of heart. If Sarah was friends with the succubus, that made it pretty clear she was no friend of mine.

Sarah's eyes widened as Anderson approached the darkened doorway. She reeled back into the shadows, but it was too late.

Anderson snatched the door open. "Who's there?" he roared.

Going on the offensive, Sarah pounced like a lion. Her aura brightened the room as she reached into a supernatural territory of power I barely understood. Its effects made me waver and my eyelids felt like hundred-pound weights suddenly hung off them. I staggered and marveled how Anderson straightened, completely unaffected by her aura. Sarah snarled and the air shifted like oil, sweeping out in a shockwave.

"Sleep!" Sarah shouted.

Anderson laughed. Damn it, he just stood there and laughed at a muse. "How kind of you to deliver yourself to my lab. You were never my main target, but since you're already here, you'll get to help me nab that succubus bitch too."

Sarah launched herself at him like a wild animal. Anderson sidestepped her attack and she landed face-first into the cement. Her lip busted and a splotch of bright red blood smeared across her cheek.

Anderson took out a pouch of tranquilizers and picked the smallest one. He kneeled over her and pricked her in the neck.

Sarah yelped and reached for the dart, but it was too late. She slumped over, completely paralyzed. But her eyes darted, still awake.

Anderson grinned and pointed his dart gun my way. The last thing I saw was Anderson dragging Sarah into my cell.

Sonya

*B*eing reminded that Sarah wasn't human wasn't what I wanted to hear right now. Nothing about my life was normal. Zack was only trying to assure me she could take care of herself, but when it came to my life, nothing ever went as planned.

I sighed and thrust out my empty glass. "Fill 'er up."

Zack smiled and popped the whiskey bottle open and poured me another drink. The wafting scent of ancient oak and orange peel tickled my nose and I brought the heat to my lips, letting it slither down and calm the butterflies in my belly.

I clicked my tongue and eyed the security guard who was pretending not to watch me. That pull between us was still there and I did the best I could to brush it off. Whoever held this connection to my runes, it certainly wasn't a human. "We almost there?" I asked the mortal, hoping to jar him out of his blatant staring.

He started and cleared his throat, then elbowed his companion who shifted to the window, pulling the drape aside. "Yes," his smooth voice replied. "We're pulling into the driveway now."

I shifted to my own window and peered outside. The limo bumped over a rail for a security gate and eased through popping gravel. Even through the heavy tinting of the glass, the array of floodlights lit up the mansion like a beacon. A Queen Anne style home blocked out the moon, and I bit my cheek in revulsion that I knew what the style was called—Sarah always said I spent far too much time watching "Million Dollar Homes."

When the limo slid to a halt, I realized I felt weak and dizzy. It wasn't the alcohol, although that didn't help. This would be the first time I was meeting a man who I not only couldn't control, but could possibly control *me*. Even Zack I could overcome to some degree. But this wasn't just a powerful incubus. This was *the* incubus. Not having my powers of seduction to fall back on made me feel more naked than if I'd dropped all my clothes and walked down a crowded beach.

Zack nudged me in the ribs and I yelped. "C'mon, succubus. It's time to get that necklace charged and get your girl back."

Once I took three steps down the grainy path, I paused to marvel at the modern castle towering over me. The mansion was just like any I'd seen on "Million Dollar Homes," and it was even more breathtaking in person. The symmetrical walls made it look like a fort, but the twirling iron bars kept it elegant. And no castle would be complete without a moat. The only way to get to the house was a narrow path flanked by a still mosaic pond on each side. As I picked my way across the stones I felt as if I'd been teleported to some outlandish Japanese garden.

A shiver of delight sped up my spine as Zack slipped an arm around my waist and guided me down the trail past the water's edge. I welcomed his warmth and was too drunk to resist pulling in the lust lingering on his skin. He only pulled me closer to his side in response, not seeming to mind that I was stealing his energy.

Zack's sexual power sobered me up just enough to keep me from staggering to the massive oak door.

"Do you think he likes blondes?" I ventured, hoping my question didn't sound as pathetic to him as it did in my own head.

Zack gave me a smile and guided me to the small screen to the side of the building. "Why don't we ask?"

I clutched his arm. "Wait. I'm not ready."

He sighed and wrapped his fingers around my hand. "What are you so nervous about?"

He drew my hand to the necklace at my chest and I let his weight linger on my breasts. Even from the minute dust I had drained from his skin, the necklace remained cold and lifeless. I wished to feel it burn again, blazing with life as it had on my mother.

I realized suddenly that I wasn't doing this for David, or Sarah. As selfish as it was, this was my chance to accept that I was a succubus. To embrace what I was, wholly and completely, and finally let go of the guilt that tormented me.

My gaze fell to my feet and I stared at the ground lamps' glow cascading across my red heels, choosing to ignore the dull bloodstains smeared across my jeans. Even if I never had to kill anyone again... could I really accept what I was? Could Sarah?

Beeps sounded as Zack plucked away on the keypad and I cried out in horror. The screen blipped on and the most beautiful creature to grace the planet smiled directly at me.

Even through the filter of pixels and the dilution of a speaker, I was instantly trapped in an iron web of magnetic desire and fascination. I could feel his heat through the screen. It didn't matter if he was a hundred feet away, at that moment I would have done anything he asked.

"Hello, you must be Sonya," he breathed and I staggered to Zack's side, grabbing onto him for stability.

So this is what my victims felt when I controlled them with their own desire.

"Would you please come in?" Derek asked and his liquid sex voice was followed by a mechanical click at the door.

I stared at the bronze handle, frozen in place.

"This place's got remote control locks. How

sweet it that?" Zack declared and gave me a hearty slap on the back and I stumbled into the screen, realizing I was pressing my breasts against the camera a bit too late.

"Oh my, aren't you friendly?" Derek's voice caressed me from the speaker.

"E-excuse me!" I launched back from the screen and gave Zack the best death glare I could manage.

"Make yourself at home," Derek continued. "I'll be down in a moment."

The screen went black and I stared at it until Zack tapped my shoulder. "You heard the man, let's go."

Zack tugged the door open and waltzed inside as if he visited the ancient, all-powerful, all *sexy* Incubus King every day of his life.

Then again, since he was just another incubus, he was unaffected by Derek's magnetism, wasn't he?

I swallowed the dry lump in my throat, wishing I'd stolen that whiskey bottle from the limo and could down it before going inside. Instead, I shook myself, fluffed my hair, and followed Zack through the doorway.

The cool air kissed my cheeks and I sighed,

not realizing how warm it'd been outside. Plus, Derek getting me all riled up and the remnants of alcohol with the buzz dried out made everything uncomfortable…and sticky.

I pulled down on the leg of my jeans as Zack disappeared around a corner.

"Hey, where you goin'?" I shouted out after him.

His voice echoed down the wide hall in reply. "He said to make ourselves at home. I'm hitting the bar!"

I snickered, and pranced across the plush maroon carpet in anticipation and my eyes scanned the massive paintings decorating the foyer. "Do you think he has more of that whiskey?"

A promising clink of glasses told me it was a good possibility. I smiled and was about to speed around the corner until the most breathtaking painting caught my eye. I enjoyed art just as much as the next girl, but something about this piece was absolutely enchanting.

A naked woman lay across a couch, and the setting seemed antiquated with long beige drapes framing a Victorian style one-armed chair. The woman, though, was draped over it as if she was absolutely timeless. The paint strokes were so intricate I could even see the wave of goose-bumps across her flawless skin. She leaned on one hand staring out into the mansion—staring straight at me.

"I see you've found Silvia," a voice breathed behind my ear and I squeaked in surprise.

Derek smiled back at me as Zack sprang into the room. His jolly gait slowed to a halt and he rubbed his neck. "Hey, man. It looks like you're out of the—"

Derek flashed Zack a wicked smile and pulled out a thick glass bottle he'd been hiding behind his back. It was even bigger than the one I'd had in the limo.

Zack laughed and produced a glass, giving me a sympathetic glance. "She's not looking too good."

I swayed, not sure what he meant. The room was a little fuzzy, and I couldn't quite focus on anything with the exception of Derek. He stood out like a beacon of clarity, as if he was the only object worthy of my attention.

Derek uncorked the whiskey bottle with his teeth and I nearly fainted with how hot *that* was.

Before I fell over, he poured and offered me the glass. "Nathan said you liked this one."

"N-Nathan?" I asked. How could he just stand there, in his half-open shirt with that massive bulge begging at the zipper of his tight jeans, and speak of someone named Nathan? Shouldn't he be wrapping his arms around my waist? Telling me I was the most beautiful creature to walk the earth, and if he didn't have me right this very moment, he'd die?

His smile broadened. "Yes, my son who you met on the ride here. He seems quite taken with you, even if he won't admit it."

I staggered against the wall, pressing myself up against Silvia's painted breast. "Your son?"

"Yes. Silva and I have had a few, actually. Too bad we haven't had a girl yet. For the boys, she can't pass on more than good looks, but," he smiled and took a white pill out of his shirt pocket, letting it *plunk* into the whiskey glass, "her looks are pretty damn good, wouldn't you agree?"

I took one long gaze at the woman in the painting peering over my shoulder. Even she seemed entranced by the Incubus King. Jealousy surged a sour taste in my mouth and I clenched my fists.

"You'll feel better after you drink this." He stretched out his arm, offering the spiked drink as I blinked furtively, battling between my desire to rip off all my clothes and ask him what the hell he put in my whiskey.

He bobbed the drink in my face. "Take it."

The Incubus King's words held a command I couldn't deny and I snatched the thick crystal from his grasp, draining the spiked drink in seconds. The whiskey burned deliciously down my throat and the knobby pill went with it.

I choked, stumbling and pressing against the painting, watching Derek suspiciously and cradling the cold glass to my breast.

Zack jolted forward. "Dude. Is she all right?"

Derek held out a hand to keep Zack quiet. "Just give her a moment."

Zack growled. "If you're messing with her I swear—"

Derek glared, sending Zack into silence.

The world spun, and it made me nervous that even Zack was worried about me. But the fact that I could even focus on him was a good sign.

After another few heavy breaths, everything became clear—the grand hall of massive paintings, the dangling crystal chandeliers, and a black-haired woman peering around a white-washed corridor who looked suspiciously like Silvia.

As if I'd imagined her, she vanished.

What was in that drink?

I shook my head as the heat in my loins abated to something less than an inferno, and my mind stopped drowning trying to imagine what was beneath Derek's pants.

Derek tilted his head with an attractive smile. "Feeling better? More..." his tongue flicked across his lips, "yourself?"

I sighed and put my face in my hands, rubbing my temples softly. "I think so." I remembered walking inside, but it felt as if I had just woken from a dream. I opened one eye to look up at him. "What'd you give me?"

"A resistant to my influence. It'll last for twenty-four hours."

I shot my head up and stared at him. "There's a drug against our powers?" I blinked. "No, more important question: Why the hell did I need a drug to think clearly around you? I'm not human." I straightened, for once indignant that my heritage didn't make me special in this situation. "I may only be twenty-two, but my mother was over five hundred years old when she had me. I should be able to resist an incubus."

Zack smiled and pulled me away from the painting and into his grasp. "He's a lot older than five hundred years. He's not called the Incubus King for his good looks alone."

With a growl I twisted my watch, fiddling with it to figure out how to set a second timer. I always felt at ease when my life timer was in the hundreds, and 724 hours and 28 minutes shown pleasantly back at me with the familiar purple glow. Managing to pop up a second timer, I set it to 24 hours before I'd be Derek-goo again.

Derek peered over my shoulder and his scent tasted like roses and sex. Even with the resistant, he exuded everything I desired.

I flicked my gaze back at him. "You don't have one?"

He hummed in response. "Can't say I've ever needed to monitor my feeding." He rested a warm hand on my shoulder and it sent butterflies fluttering back to life in my stomach. "Only those of us who deny ourselves need such devices."

Zack pulled me away from Derek and closer into his chest. "That's my sister. She cares about the humans, you know." He kissed the back of my head. "She waits until she finds someone willing to die for her rather than simply take what she needs."

Derek chuckled, but it wasn't in a mocking way. "I admire that."

I wriggled out of Zack's grasp, even though it felt familiar and safe. I needed to focus on my mission. Charge the necklace. Save David. Win Sarah back.

My manicured hand shot to the lifeless silver around my neck. "I'm here to charge this. Zack said you knew an incubus who could help."

Zack offered a muffled chuckle and I glowered at him. What was so damn funny?

Derek's eyelashes lowered and considered the locket. He drifted his fingers over it, and a soft warmth encased the metal at his touch. "I believe I can help you with that." Just when I caught the gleam in his eye and realized he meant *he* was the one who was going to charge my necklace, his smile turned wicked. "You'll need to do something for *me* first."

I narrowed my gaze and glared at Derek. I

needed the necklace charged. I needed to save David if I was ever to live with myself, or see Sarah again. "What do I have to do?"

He bent down to press his lips against my ear. "Fuck my wife."

ANDERSON'S TRUTH

Luke

When I woke, Sarah was seething in the corner. Anderson had left the lights on and looked far too smug slicing his apple while lounging on a puke-green chair.

Anderson narrowed his eyes at his newest prisoner. "I'm not quite sure what species you are yet."

"Doesn't much matter." Sarah glared. "You resisted my powers, not that it should be possible."

He shrugged. "I have a knack for supernaturals. It's the same way I can resist your succubus friend, I suppose." He leaned on his knees. "Look.

I don't think I'm human either, but unlike you two," he pointed the knife, "I don't have any nifty powers to separate me from the rest. I just... resist." His palm layed out flat, as if that wasn't any sort of personal achievement.

Sarah rolled her eyes. "That's a damn good power, if you ask me. So, what do you want with us?"

He glanced at me. "I need all the power I can get to rescue my daughter."

His daughter? The psycho had offspring? What an unfortunate blight on the world. I hoped I'd never meet the she-beast.

"You could try asking for help," Sarah suggested.

He frowned, and then stood. He unbuttoned his suit and pulled his shirt until we were plagued with the pasty white of his ribcage. A nasty red scar lit across his side. "This is what I got when I tried asking." He tucked his shirt back in.

I couldn't take it anymore and beat my fists against the bars. One puny little scar and he'd justified kidnapping and torture? Just because I didn't keep a scar didn't mean I didn't have a vendetta too. He'd sliced me up like an onion on a daily basis and I was going to kill him one day. Nice and slow.

"Calm down, freak," Anderson barked. "I know you don't have any sympathy for me. But I don't need it. Once I get the succubus, you're free to go."

That was news to me. If he thought I'd just shake his hand and be on my way, he had another thing coming.

Sarah frowned. "What's Sonya got to do with this?"

He smiled. "You know, freak here never asked. But I think you'd appreciate what I'm trying to do." He settled himself into his chair like a fluffed out hen. "A succubus can extract power, right? And I resist it." He leaned, his eyes growing wide and intense. "She kissed me, once. When she thought her powers worked on me. Do you know what happened next? I realized I wasn't human, because I woke up ten years younger and my wife was dead." A moment of rage passed his face. "Unfortunately, by the time I figured it all out, the succubus was long gone and so was my daughter." His eyes narrowed. "I've been tracking her ever since. The Black Widow. That's what I called her when I saw what she did to men." Anderson went quiet and his gaze drifted to David.

Sarah turned somber as we considered his slow-rising chest.

"She can't just get away with this. I'm going to take her abilities again, and I'm not going to take life with it. I'm going to take power." His eyes met mine. "I'm going to take every supernatural's power I can and save my daughter."

Sarah scoffed. "Take a supernatural's power? Sonya can't do that."

He popped a slice of apple into his mouth. "I can do it. I just need a boost." He eyed me like a hungry beast. "Infinite regeneration would be a pretty convenient power to have. It'd get me a long way towards rescuing my daughter if I could recover from dagger wounds." He shrugged. "I'm not the best in a knife fight."

Sarah glanced at me. "Regeneration, huh?" She searched my eyes, and then her own went wide as if a memory had been triggered. Shit. She knows what I am?

She coughed politely, turning her head away. "Never heard of a supernatural who could regenerate."

Anderson waved his knife. "No matter. I just

need to get the succubus to turn herself in and then my real experiments can get started."

I scoffed. Anderson shot me a glare. "Aw, don't be jealous. I'm not done with you yet." His grin turned sinister. "You still have your role to play."

Anderson glanced at David and frowned. The poor guy had deterioration something fierce, and being locked in a cell without food wasn't helping matters. "First one to let me know when he finally wakes up gets dinner."

With that he switched off the lights and left the room.

I shivered in the darkness. I'd gotten used it, but now there were two other people in the room. I didn't like being unable to see them, especially when one was in the same cell as me. And she also happened to be a muse.

I jumped when her hand rested on my shoulder.

"Hey," she said. "Sorry. I just…" She went silent. I pulled away but then she grabbed my shoulder again. "Hold still. I feel something."

My whole body went rigid as a surge of power bit into my skin. The bitch was strong. I'd give her that. Her aura seeped into me like a cold shard of ice. I'd never felt anything quite like it. I wanted to say, "Get off me, bitch. I get enough stab wounds from Anderson." But nothing other than a pathetic groan came out.

The razor retreated and she pulled away. "Holy shit."

I backed into the bars and slumped. If she wanted to tell me what she'd found, she would.

Her breaths went heavy. "I see why your mother didn't tell you what you were. You weren't ready." She sighed. "You're still not ready. But you will be when this is all over."

There it was again. Everyone else seemed to know so much about me, yet I was kept in the dark. Anderson's cell was just a metaphor for my life. When would the lights turn on? What was this promise of "when it was over?" Would it really ever end?

"You have a key to this cell," she whispered. "You can leave whenever you want."

I stiffened. Yes. I did have a key to my cell. I kept it hidden under a loose stone in the back wall. One of the police officials who was not as corrupt as Anderson had thought had given it to me. But I couldn't leave, not until I'd fulfilled my mother's vision. I had to endure this until the woman came to me.

I expected Sarah to rush to the back wall and undo all my work. If she used the key to escape, Anderson would know and I'd never have an escape plan for when it was time to leave. I crouched, ready to stop her and do whatever I needed to do. I'd already endured more torture than any man alive and I wasn't going to let a muse fuck this up.

"I understand," was all Sarah said. I relaxed, but still didn't trust her. I ran my hand against the bars and made my way to the wall, slumping down against the loose stone. If she was trying to trick me, she'd have to get past my body first. But she didn't make a move. Instead, I heard her make her way to the opposite corner of the cell and sit down. And then we drifted off into sleep, listening to David's slow breaths engulf the silence.

A DOUBLE-D COCKTAIL

Sonya

"Excuse me?" I asked, a bit surprised by his request. Incubus or not, what kind of man asked someone to screw his wife?

He tugged at my sleeve and Zack reluctantly let me go.

"Aw, don't look so glum, my friend. I'm not going to take Sonya without leaving you something in return." Derek clapped his hands twice.

Movement caught my eye down the corridor where I thought I'd seen Silva.

Three girls wearing bikinis covered in sheer pink dresses flounced out of the hall full of giggles and smiles. "Derek!" they squealed in unison.

I rolled my eyes. Nothing I hated more than mindless thralls.

Zack, however, perked up. "Hey, chicas!" He spread his arms as if he expected the girls to frolic into his embrace, scantily clad boobs and all.

Instead, they flounced right past Zack and draped over Derek, pulling at his already half-open shirt and revealing a set of six-pack abs that just wouldn't quit.

Zack's arms fell and his mouth drooped into a pout.

A red-head stood on her tippy-toes and flicked her tongue against Derek's earlobe. "What can we do for you, master?"

Derek shrugged the girls off as if they were pests. "You're for Zack."

They frowned, and the blonde hugging his waist scrunched her nose. "But we want *you*."

Zack sighed. "Man. I can't compete when you're in the room."

Derek laughed. "They'll be fine once I leave." He peeled the girls off his chest. "Okay, ladies. Wait here and I promise you'll find Zack more appealing once I'm gone." Derek winked at me and took my hand. "I have something else on the menu tonight."

I swallowed. I'd never had a threesome before. Not that I was opposed to the idea, but it was bad enough I'd kill one person, let alone two. Needless to say, I'd never found an Incubus King and his wife for such an opportunity to present itself.

I let Derek lead me away while the other girls gave me angry stares. Their interest waned once we'd made our way down the hall and they investigated Zack with increasing cascades of giggles. He offered me an encouraging wave as Derek swept me around the corner.

"I imagine you've never done something like this before," Derek said. I nodded and he squeezed my hand. "I'm not going to make you do anything you don't want to do. That's why I gave you a dose of Silvia's blood." He bobbed his head to the side, as if to admit that was only a half-truth. "Well, that and I need you capable of looking at Silvia instead of me."

I blinked. "Silvia's... blood?" A wave of queasiness swept through my stomach. I'd told Maxine I wasn't a vampire. I wasn't... right?

"It's not easy to make a dose. But I won't get into the technicalities of how it all works." He pointed to a door at the end of the long corridor encrusted with silver. "Those are my bedchambers."

I blinked and reluctantly tugged away from him. "Look, I'm sorry but I'm confused." I wrapped my fingers around the cold necklace. "I need to charge this. Someone's life is on the line and it's my fault. I can do whatever you want later... but first, please, help me charge this and undo my mistake."

He chuckled, running a finger under my chin. "My dear, you and your necklace can have all the sexual energy my wife has to offer. I don't need it." His finger ran down my throat and traced a circle around the locket across my cleavage. "My wife isn't human. I don't know what she is, actually, but she can charge this without even breaking a sweat." He bent, placing his lips on the locket and warmth pressed through to my chest.

Even with the resistant, my knees turned to Jell-O and I couldn't help but bite my lip in anticipation, my eyes glued to his hairless pecs.

I forced myself to match his gaze, and he smirked. How could a smirk be so damn hot? His skin reminded me of silk on marble and I couldn't help but graze my finger across his collarbone. I'd never wanted something so bad and wanted to run away at the same time. Derek was a "double D" cocktail: delicious... and dangerous.

What the hell am I getting myself into?

"I'm not sure what to expect," I said.

"Come with me and you can see for yourself."

I suddenly felt anxious and unsure. Is this something I really wanted to do?

"Why don't you tell me a little bit more about your wife first?" I leaned against the wall and crossed my arms. "She's got to be something special if you've got a giant ass painting of her naked for everyone to see in your living room."

Derek chuckled. "She's not shy." He straightened, tucking the tips of his fingers into his waistband. "She's the mother of my children. She's an endless supply of love, life, and sexual energy."

I cocked my head to the side. A sense of hope swept over me. "Endless? She doesn't experience deterioration?"

"No. I've never seen anything like her in all my years." His gaze grew distant and my hope dwindled. It was too good to be true. I'd have to continue to kill to survive, unless I found someone like her. He said she could charge the Blood Stone. Did that mean I could feed off her? I couldn't simply start up a tryst with the Incubus King's wife... or could I?

As if he sensed my malicious thoughts, he leaned in with a growl in his throat. "Let's get something straight. You're just here to do what I need you to do. When the night's done, she's mine."

My knees went weak and I swallowed a dry lump in my throat, wishing I had more whiskey to endure the fire burning in Derek's eyes. "You're pretty good at reading body language," I said with a weak laugh, hoping flattery would buy me some kudos. His stare continued to bore through me. "If you're so protective, why do you want me to sleep with her? I don't get it."

He sighed, rubbing the back of his neck. I relaxed, feeling as if he'd lowered his hackles. "She's kind of...more into chicks." His face went red-hot.

I blinked. "What?"

He looked down the hall at the silver encrusted door, his face drooping. "I know she loves me. And she wants children just as much as I do, which is probably why she stays with me at all." His gaze drifted to the necklace resting atop my breasts. "But the way it works is she can't become pregnant if she's not aroused. I'm not sure why, or how, but that's just the way her body is built."

I choked on a laugh and rushed a hand to my face. "Sorry," I blurted the apology and turned sober. "You have no effect on her?"

He eyed me as if he was tired. "Her blood makes the resistant, remember? And if she's a lesbian at heart, it's not easy for me to get her blood pumping."

I hummed. I may only be twenty-two years old, but I'd never once heard of a creature, human or otherwise, who could resist the Incubus King.

"So, why do you need me?" I peered down the way we had come. "What of those thralls?"

His eyes went dark. "Do you really think I want to conceive my child by taking someone else's life? No, I need a succubus. And there aren't many of your kind left, nor many willing to take the risk."

I jerked upright. "What risk?"

He waved the air as if my question had no merit. "Your necklace will protect you from that."

I pulled the collar of his shirt, hearing a slight rip of the silk as I pulled him to look me in the eye. "What…risk?"

He smiled, his hot breath puffing on my face in a short laugh. "Have you ever heard of a succubus overfeeding?"

I released his collar. "No."

He placed one hand against the wall next to my head and leaned in, and I suddenly became aware of his hard chest so close to mine. "I learned it the hard way. Our first try with a succubus left her mad with the surplus sexual energy. I'd been so afraid of depriving her that I'd given her too much, and she drowned in it. A bit ironic, wouldn't you say?"

I swallowed and averted my eyes, then flicked them back when I'd registered what he'd just said. "What do you mean *you* gave her too much? It's your wife's sexual energy, how is it yours to give?" I shifted my weight and tried to ignore Derek's hot breath tickling my neck. "It's one thing to push sexual energy onto humans, but it's quite another to transfer it to another succubus. I should know, trying to feed off

Zack is like getting three drops of water from a stone. Is that some Incubus King perk or something?"

Derek pushed in closer with an impatient growl, groping across my flat stomach. I froze when his fingers grazed mercilessly over my runes. They awoke under his touch, blazing with heat and he flinched. His hand groped until he reached the rune that seemed to blend with his warmth on the far left of my ribcage.

He tried to lift my shirt to get a better look, but I gripped his wrist and widened my eyes. He was one of the seven, somehow, just like Sarah had been. I felt a kindred strength and his link to my destiny—but not one of the *four*—whatever the fuck that meant. There was something sinister there, too, but I needed to explore why my prophecy included him. I needed to know why my body sang under him. "Do you feel that?" I asked, both hesitant and hopeful.

His fingers continued to stroke and he leaned in until his breath caressed my skin. "What is it?" he asked, sounding curious now.

"You and I..." I breathed, "we share a destiny."

He laughed—actually fucking laughed at me —then his teeth bit into my neck and I held in the moan of pleasure. "I don't believe in destiny," he growled.

I straightened, pushing him back and stepping purposefully for the bedchambers. "All right. Let's get on with it then, shall we? I have a human to save and you have a wife to get pregnant." He might believe in destiny, but my stupid ass runes didn't just light up for anyone.

He gave me a wicked smile, seeming pleased with my eagerness. "Am I wrong, or are you more into women yourself?"

I offered him a dry chuckle, wrapping my fingers around the silver handle. "I suppose we'll find out."

SILVIA

Sonya

*I*f I'd thought the painting in Derek's foyer was breathtaking, then seeing Silvia in the flesh was like a 3D hologram on the sexual equivalent of steroids. She rose from the bed, her flawless skin covered only by a skimpy nightgown and a layer of lace ribbing across her chest underneath. Only a perfect figure could pull off such a tight stretch of fabric. Derek had said she wasn't shy, but damn, I wasn't sure even I could wear a getup like that.

As she glided across the room, her shadow crawling across the beige marble and curling about my feet, I wondered if she was ever allowed outside. The moon formed a halo around her head, making her look like Lilith, an immortal succubus I'd heard about in fairy tales. And if I'd seen Silvia on the street, I'd think her Lilith incarnate.

"You must be Silvia." I extended my hand in greeting. "I'm Sonya. Pleased to meet you."

Her plump lips curved into a wry smile. "Aren't you formal?" Her words held a mysterious accent that melted my heart.

She bypassed my hand and swept into my chest, wrapping her arms around my torso and pressing her lips against my cheek. I chuckled, folding my arms around her body and letting my fingers tease the curled strands of the midnight-colored locks bouncing all the way down to her waist. Her scent enveloped me, springing up images of fresh peeled oranges and orchids.

But I couldn't ignore a cold sensation that filled my heart. Like any other woman on this planet, I couldn't feel any of her sexual energy.

I pulled away, feeling naked even though I was fully clothed. She smiled, her cheeks flushed and her long eyelashes drooping over her emerald eyes in a flirtatious flutter.

"How do you like her, my dear?" Derek asked his wife, his words dripping with lust and hope.

Silvia giggled, and the sound chimed against my ears as the most pleasant sound to have ever existed. "She's perfect."

My thumb ran around the ring on my pinky out of habit. While her words were kind, I couldn't sense any energy on her skin. Even with Sarah I felt *something*. "She doesn't seem to like me."

Derek chuckled knowingly, draping his arms over the both of us and pulling me into his chest...and closer to Silvia's lips.

"I assure you," Derek said, "you're quite mistaken."

I'd never seen sexual energy as a visible aura before, but in my gut I felt Derek do something and the air around us snapped. His right hand glowed blue as it squeezed Silvia's shoulder, the light crawling through his veins until it made its way to the other side...and into me.

I gasped with the sensation of Silvia's desire. Silvia moaned and the sexual energy burned through my skin where Derek held on tight. I leaned in, placing my lips against hers, and reveled in the burn of her lust and the silk of her skin. Now, I understood. I could never feed off of a woman. It was a limitation spun by the cruel gods who had created my race. But with Derek as a conduit, I could bend the rules.

Like a funnel, the sexual energy saturated my skin and bones until it migrated into my necklace, filling it like an endless reservoir.

My hands groped across the tight lace binding her abdomen and pulled at the strings. The bodice loosened just enough for me to reach my hand in-between her thighs. Still locked in a kiss, I grinned against her teeth when I felt the moist welcome of my touch.

A pulse ran through Derek's hand and he staggered. His stiff erection rolled against my leg and suddenly I was very aware of the magnitude of his presence. Silvia was no succubus, but her allure was fascinating. Thanks to Derek, I could feel it for myself. He'd opened a whole new world to me and my hand fell to his erection, wishing to show my gratitude.

Derek chuckled and removed his grip. My body went cold without access to Silvia's lust and I cried out. "No, please. Don't take it away."

Derek gave Silvia a fond smile. "All yours, my dear."

Her hands caressed my breasts and ran down to the rim of my shirt, tugging it off my body. I complied, wishing only to feel her desire again. She paused as she examined my runes. I kept a hand on the one Derek had activated and its heat threatened to burn me, but I kept my grip. She finally smiled, appeased with what looked no more to be than tattoos, and she pushed down my pants. Now naked, I shivered in the cool air. Silvia led me to the bed as Derek disrobed.

She lay down on her back and pulled me on top of her, safely hiding the rune between the shadow of our bodies. As my tongue danced with hers, a shock of heat hit me from behind. Derek's erection fit between my butt cheeks and Silvia stretched her hands around my neck. When Derek and Silvia grasped wrists, any contact with Derek's skin set me on fire. I gasped and lowered my hips, grinding against Silvia. Her moan was intoxicating. Derek eased inside of me carefully, as if he was afraid to break the fragile connection between the three of us. I pushed my hips back and he slid in farther. I gasped again, feeling Silvia's stimulation against mine, and Derek filling me up from the inside. We all moved together as if we were one. My necklace burned hot with the rolling waves of sexual energy bursting through my body.

The rocking escalated, forcing me over the cliff of an orgasm that threatened to take me under. Derek only kept moving, easily taking my contractions and pounded into me without relent.

Silvia was about to reach her climax, which through our connection I knew was a rare occurrence. Every thrust sent me rolling stimulation over her. Yet it wasn't just the touch, but the sensation of oneness we had with each other. It was only amplified by the power of the rune across my side that recognized Derek as a piece of my destiny, one of the seven, and a sin that would help me avoid the looming darkness that had haunted me all my life.

Her eyes fluttered closed and Silvia bit her plump lip until her lips parted in a soft gasp. Derek felt it too. With one swift motion he pulled out of me and thrust into his wife. I was pushed into her breasts and could hardly endure the level of sexual power radiating through Derek's hard grip against my shoulders.

As she cried out in climax and he came into her, I felt the explosion as if I were him, leaving my seed and my hope for a future inside her womb. I felt her wish, and his, as if they were my own. There would be a child. The knowledge of the power of our union brought me to tears and I cried out with them, feeling the full effects of their euphoria. When the tremors slowed, I slumped over Silvia's heaving body, and Derek rested over mine, not pulling out of his wife. I wanted that moment to last forever, and so did they. And when I managed to open my eyes and look down, Silvia's sweat-glistened breasts were pressed against mine, illuminated by the intense glow of the locket containing the Blood Stone. We'd done it. I now had enough power to save David, face the truth of my prophecy, and live my life without feeding... for now.

SARAH'S SACRIFICE

Luke

David's bloodcurdling scream sent shivers down my spine. Where was his succubus now? Did she even care what he was going through because she'd spread her legs?

"Stop moving," Anderson chided. "Freak doesn't put up such a fuss."

I rolled my eyes and tested my wrists against the straps. I was lying flat on the good ol' torture table. Just one of those cold metal gurneys you'd see in a morgue. It made me envy a corpse.

Anderson patted me on the shoulder and his fingers stuck to my skin, glued with David's blood as the adhesive. I jerked away, as much as I could with my body strapped to the gurney.

"Stop it!" Sarah shrieked. She wasn't laid out like David and me. Anderson had tied her to one of those puke-green office chairs supposedly to keep an eye on her. Though if you asked me, he just got kicks out of having an audience.

Anderson waved the scalpel at her. "He's dead anyway. No sense letting him waste away when he could do some good in this world."

David moaned, all sense torn out from him after Anderson had sliced open his chest. He should have passed out by now, but there was magic in his veins to dull the pain. I couldn't imagine how much the deterioration would hurt otherwise without the magical numbing. I would have appreciated the succubus not leaving her victim to suffer, if I hadn't been pissed at her for making David a victim in the first place.

Anderson picked up the rib spreader. Thanks to this place being some kind of bioresearch center, he had all kinds of tools to rip a body open. He fumbled with the crank, holding it up to the light. Did he even know how to use the damn thing?

"You're going to kill him!" Sarah shouted and

clanked against her chair. It fell over and she cried out.

Anderson laughed. "No. I won't be the one to kill him." He tilted the rib spreader and the sheen of metal glinted against the fluorescent light. A cruel grin spread across his face before he lowered it into David's open chest.

David gasped in panic, his fingers trembling and his eyes locked on the crank. I wished he'd just pass out already.

Anderson's face turned hard. I knew that look of determination. It's how he looked every time he maimed me. My supernatural "gifts" rarely let me pass out either.

When I heard the sickening *crack* of David's ribs being spread, I turned my face and vomited. Anderson could do all kinds of shit to me, but I would heal. What he was doing to David was permanent.

Sarah began to sob and hot tears pricked my eyes. I didn't know David very well, but he seemed like a half decent guy. He didn't deserve this.

When the screams stopped, I turned back to see if David was dead. He'd passed out, thankfully, and Anderson had his hand *inside* David's chest. But that wasn't the worst part. Anderson was glowing.

At first, I thought it was a trick of the light. But his skin had an unmistakable red hue, and blue streaks were spidering up his veins.

"It's working!" Anderson shrieked.

Once the blue essence had run all the way up to Anderson's shoulder, he took out his bloodied hand. The maniac was actually onto something. Our powers were kept within our hearts. Or at least, the succubus's curse had settled there in David.

He grinned and his wild gaze caught mine. "Time for the real test."

As he reached for me, lust for power filling his gaze, Sarah thwacked him from behind. Anderson yelped out in pain. "Bitch!"

Sarah's wrists dripped with blood, the result of yanking herself free of the plastic ties. She balled her hands into fists, ready to fight. "If you think I'm letting you steal Luke's powers, you're insane."

Anderson laughed. "Ah, told you his name did he? You two getting chatty? Close?"

Sarah swung with an impressive right hook with a grunt and Anderson leaped out of the way. The air shimmered as she delved into her powers.

He laughed. "Your powers don't work on me."

But her powers hadn't been aimed at Anderson. Strength surged through my arms, enough to break my binds. I'd never imagined a muse was capable of anything like that.

I burst off the gurney and pummeled towards Anderson. He swiveled and reached in his pocket for the tranq gun. But I dove on him and began beating him in the face. Blind rage overtook me. I didn't care about my mother's vision or saving the world. I didn't care if I lived or died. All I wanted to do was beat the shit out of that man.

Then Anderson pierced me in the chest with a cold iron rod. It went straight through, nearly grazing my heart, and I doubled over as I vomited up blood. Then a cold chill swept through me, not from blood loss, but Anderson's stolen magic seeping into my skin, looking for my powers to drain.

Sarah swept in and pushed me off. The rod yanked out of my chest and I gasped. Through bleary eyes I watched in horror as Anderson took a dagger and plunged it into Sarah's bosom. Anderson smiled as her ice-blue eyes turned dull and grey. Her eyelids fluttered and I knew he'd taken her powers instead of mine.

Anderson grinned and looked my way. "Get back on the table." The command hit me hard. And before I knew it, I'd done exactly as he'd said.

TAKES ONE TO KNOW ONE

Sonya

*W*aking up in the king-sized bed wrapped in maroon velvet sheets gave me a terrifying jolt of panic. This was exactly how I'd imagined I'd die. I froze, sure that the wet warmth running down my lips was my own blood. Everything felt hot and slick with my own sweat. With a stab of fear, I groped across my stomach, looking for the protruding hilt of a knife impaled by a retaliating lover. Instead, I found Silvia's warm hand draped around my waist just above the rune that had stitched over with cool, pink skin. Whatever Derek had given me, my runes were satisfied.

With a sigh of relief, I wiped the drool from my mouth and peeled off Silvia's fingers, surprised at the weight until I realized Derek's arm was on top of hers. Both stirred, smiling with half-closed eyes as I crawled out of the bed.

Silvia, with her long gorgeous hair sprawled across the pillow, was the most beautiful creature I'd ever seen. Her breasts bunched up like they were stuck in a corset made by Derek's weight, the good bits hidden by his muscular arm. I'd gotten more than an eyeful in the mystical aura of the Blood Stone, but craved to see if she was really that perfect in the stark reality of dawn.

Derek closed his eyes, settling around his wife with a satisfied sigh and his arm slipped. My heart leaped and I bit my lip. Yep. Definitely perfect.

Silvia didn't mind me looking at her. She seemed to enjoy the scrutiny as my gaze lingered on her skin. But when I met her gaze, I couldn't look away. Her eyes were so grey they seemed silver, and she hardly looked human by the way her cheekbones arched a bit too high. She kept her magnificent eyes on mine, and her mouth formed a silent "thank you."

A blush rose to my cheeks. How was she the one thanking me? But as she groped across her stomach and held it there, I realized. Last night I was hit so hard with their elation of a child. But with a heritage like that, what kind of child would it be, especially if it was a girl?

Silvia glanced at my necklace just for the briefest of moments, her face becoming a rainbow of emotions I couldn't decipher. Then she reached for the nightstand, tugging open the drawer. She flashed me a smile and gestured to it before settling back into the sheets. She pulled her husband's arm around her body and tucked his hand under her ribs like a child's blanket and closed her eyes.

Free from the magnetizing hold of Silvia's gaze, and afresh with curiosity, I peered into the open drawer. A simple purple drawstring pouch was the only object, and when I opened it, a single white pill rested inside.

It was one of Silvia's blood pills, a resistant, and for some reason... she wanted me to have it.

I wrapped my fingers around the prize and gave the sleeping couple one more glance. Last night had been draining for both of them; and I was the only one left with energy. And damn, there was so much energy! My limbs tingled and I wanted to do a hundred jumping jacks and then run twenty miles. And it wasn't just from the sheer amount of energy I'd been fed, but the realization I was waking up and the person next to me wouldn't have to die.

Resisting the urge to clap my hands like a delighted child who'd learned not to kill caterpillars, I drew a deep breath and took in the luxury of the bedroom. The morning light revealed ridiculous amounts of crystal absorbing dawn's rays, only to spit them out again in blinks of white. The ceiling dripped with glass like we were inside a cave with stalactites that grew nothing but jewels and diamonds. Even the walls glittered, and I became dizzy with the richness of it all. Who had the kind of money to bedazzle their entire room?

I supposed an Incubus King, and his succubus-feeding wife.

Finding my jeans draped across an oak chest, I snatched them up and grimaced at the sight of the dried blood across the denim. I really needed to get home and find a change of clothes. Did I have enough detergent to get day-old blood stains out?

The reality of life hit me then, thinking of laundry and my apartment and such regular things. Sarah was out there... and David could be saved.

My hand shot to my necklace, finding it scalding hot. The skin around my cleavage had grown accustomed to the warmth, but my fingertips were cold and clammy from lying on top of the covers, exuding the heat from the night's exertions. I bounced the locket from one hand to the other until my hands warmed, and popped it open.

The Blood Stone radiated as if I'd set a ruby on fire. The energy in the gem swirled, roiling like a gleaming whirlpool. I'd never seen a Blood Stone this alive.

I clicked the locket closed and the moment of awe passed. Nausea set in, thinking of what Derek had said last night of a succubus dying from overfeeding. What would have happened to me if I didn't have an empty Blood Stone for protection? Did Derek fear for his own life? Is that why he didn't hold back, and gave me all Silvia had to offer?

Questions for another day. I had a man to save, and sins to amend with Sarah.

I donned last night's clothes, slipped on my heels, and eased out of the room.

Clicking my way through the empty hall, I realized I wasn't exactly sure where David would be. Of course, he'd be with Detective Anderson. But where was that pest hiding now? He wouldn't still be at his old rundown office. I'd had Zack ransack that place more than once.

Turning around the last bend of the hall, I found Zack wearing nothing but his jeans. He teetered on the edge of an enormous leather chair, failing to procure any of the expensive comfort as he leaned on his elbows and stared at his phone. He balanced on the balls of his feet, bouncing his heels on the ground, never taking his gaze off the screen.

"Shouldn't you be in bed with a bunch of thrall girls or something?" I asked, pinching my cheek between my teeth.

He glanced at me. "It's not polite to speak of the dead."

I balked. "What?"

He shrugged and looked back at his phone. "What can I say. I was hungry."

There was a certain fondness for Zack in my heart. But it was times like these that I was reminded how true he was to our race. He saw humans as food. Nothing more. Nothing less. I could never truly love anyone who felt that way.

As always, I attempted to divert my feelings with humor. "Waking up next to a corpse is the least sexy thing I can think of. Much less three."

He glared. "You're one to talk." He thrust the phone at me like a spear.

Blinking, I took it and stared at the screen.

A message from Sarah. My heart lifted, until I read what it said.

I have my evidence, and the freak of a girlfriend.

The Black Widow has 24 hours to turn herself in, or the girlfriend's next.

- Detective A.

*T*wo pictures were attached, and I tapped the screen while my heart fluttered its way up my throat.

. . .

*T*he first image was a close-up of Sarah, gagged, with one black eye, and a frightening patch of red around her chest, holding up a note that read, "4112 Lance Street. Come in 24 hours or I die."

The second image was loaded off the screen and my finger trembled as I scrolled to see what came next.

Bile rose in my throat when I saw David had fully deteriorated. His pasty grey skin was taut across his cheeks and his cloudy eyes stared back at me, full of judgment and terror.

David was dead.

*T*he phone clattered to the ground as tears welled in my eyes. "D-David. How is he dead?"

Zack wouldn't look at me. Rage filled my chest and I stomped towards him and shook a clenched fist. "Don't you sit there and judge me. You just killed three innocent girls. *Three!*"

"Thralls choose their fate, David didn't."

There was truth in that. A selection of humans learned what we were, and what would happen to them if they slept with one of us. There was nothing short of a cult, full of an endless supply of men and women who thought it an honor to give their life-force to a supernatural. They told themselves that they'd be reborn as a succubus or incubus themselves, but that's not how the curse worked. There was no rebirth. There was only death.

Zack had the nerve to roll his eyes before he stood. My fist went flying of its own accord, aimed straight at his face.

Zack could have dodged, but he didn't. My knuckles cracked against his cheekbone and a shockwave rippled through the air. My ears popped and the hairs on my arms singed from the heat.

How dumb could I be? I'd just filled a Blood Stone to the brim. My locket and body burned with more sexual energy than I'd ever had in my life, and Zack had just devoured three thralls. No way would we be able to hurt each other.

A breath shuddered into my lungs and I shook my fist as if it hurt, but it only felt hot.

Two knuckle marks seared red across his

skin before vanishing. Zack watched me, his own fists clenched and his lips curled over his teeth in a snarl. He was always laughing. I wasn't used to seeing him this way. I tensed, waiting for him to retaliate, but he relaxed his shoulders and waited for my heaving breaths to slow before he spoke. "Sonya," he whispered my name. "How much time did you have left when you slept with David?"

"What?"

He glanced at my watch. "You always time your starvation down to the millisecond. How close was it?"

I swallowed. What did that matter?

His eyes went wide. "How close?"

"Seconds," I spat.

He clicked his tongue and looked away. "The fuck, Sonya."

"That shouldn't have mattered. I was with him for not even half an hour. There's no way that was enough to kill him, no matter how hungry I was. He should've had months left." I crawled my fingers through my tangled hair and growled with frustration. "How is he dead?"

Zack's hand rested on my arm and I flung him off. I couldn't stand for anyone to touch me right now. I shouldn't have left David alone with that madman. While I was having orgasmic, supernatural sex... David...

"Detective Anderson must have done something," Zack blurted.

I matched his gaze and held onto it, searching for some grain of hope that this wasn't all my fault.

His hand hovered over my arm, but then his fingers retracted, curling into a ball. "If he's got Sarah then we were wrong about everything. Your powers aren't to blame."

I swallowed. Sarah was still in danger. But she was a muse. She should be able to protect herself. My mind reeled back to the image of her with a black eye and that blood spot pooled just above her stomach. It didn't seem real.

"Look," Zack said, splitting into my thoughts again. "This is bigger than Sarah. If that detective has got something that can mess with our powers, we need to find out what it is. This puts our entire race in danger. You understand what that means?"

I'd never heard of anyone finding a way to mess with our powers. But the few times I'd come face-to-face with that damned detective, he'd been unaffected by my touch. I'd just assumed something was wrong with me...

My gaze fell to the floor. The phone was still laying there like road kill. Its black screen reflected the image of the paintings lining the wall. Silvia's was right in front of us, and I hadn't even noticed the shockwave had dotted it with bits of smoldering embers. *Derek is going to kill me...*

Zack's hands wrapped around my shoulders and I squeezed my eyes shut.

"Get ahold of yourself. You have a *Blood Stone*. We can save Sarah, and stop that stupid human."

I wriggled out of his grasp with a snarl of anguish. "We? There is no 'we' here. You don't give two shits about humans, probably muses either. I'm going to save Sarah, and I'm going alone." I whirled and stomped for the massive double-doors. Placing both hands on the oak, my rage exuded through my skin and seared burn marks on the wood.

"Sonya." Zack's voice was hardly above a whisper.

"What?" I snapped.

Zack's heat lingered at my back, but he didn't attempt to touch me. "Be careful."

There was no way I was going to respond to that. If I wasn't a succubus, he wouldn't have cared what happened to me. His love was hollow, and *wrong*. I deserved better than that.

Rage swelled in my chest, turning my locket molten hot and jolting energy through my fingertips like lightning. Spider cracks flew through the doors, the wood turning black before splintering under my weight. Sunlight poured in, far too cheerful for my mood. I snarled at it before walking outside, and head towards 4112 Lance Street.

BROKEN HEARTS

Luke

My own screams reverberated in my head. Sarah sobbed somewhere in the background, yet at the same time it was as if she was here, right in front of me.

Anderson poised the scalpel before slicing and plunged his fingers into my chest. The agony reverberated through my body and burned like fire. Then I felt what I had hoped was just my imagination. Anderson had Sarah's powers. They'd altered, and weren't as strong, but I could feel the magic within him. The magic whispered to me, urging me to hand over my powers to

Anderson. Even if I wanted to, I couldn't obey. My powers weren't something to trade. They were simply a part of me.

Anderson snarled. "Dammit!"

I gasped when he jerked his hand out and blood trailed down my ribs.

Through my bleary vision I could make out Anderson waving the bloody scalpel at Sarah. "I only had enough to absorb one supernatural's power! I didn't want yours. It's useless!"

Sarah spat.

Anderson sneered and turned back to me. "Come on, freak. Give me your powers."

I'd do anything to make the agony end. I babbled incoherently and Anderson didn't bother to try and understand. He went straight to work plucking out bits of my body, forcing it to scramble into regeneration. I jerked and the IV sticking out of my vein tugged at my wrist. The cold fluid seeped into my body, replacing the blood I was losing by the pint. Anderson gave me a short reprieve as he replaced the bag, tossed it to a building pile on the floor. The damn guy wouldn't let me wither up and die. He'd keep this regeneration going on forever.

He continued his work, slicing off my ear and holding his hand over the flesh as it grew back. Magic tingled across my forming veins, and added its own burn to my plethora of pain. Yet I kept regenerating, which meant Anderson wasn't getting any closer to absorbing my powers.

Anderson tossed the scalpel and it clattered across the floor. "There must be a way!" He stomped his foot like a child having a tantrum. "I have to be able to replicate it! I can't risk the bitch getting the best of me. Just one fuck up and I'm done for." For the first time, he hesitated. Desperation flashed across his glassy eyes and then all the color drained from his face. He stepped to the tool table and took the rib spreader once again, still stained with David's lifeblood.

I strained against my binds. But I was so weak and so cold. Anderson had taken off all my clothes just so he could slice up every inch of my skin. The small slits had already sealed. But the larger gash running up my chest strained to close. Anderson forced the rib spreader in before it could.

He pumped the crank once and a crack reverberated through my chest. I screamed, but the mere sound of my own voice could hardly express that sensation. I'd never been so horrified in my life. He was literally ripping me apart.

Another pump of the crank sent me into manic cries for the pain to end. For the sweet darkness of death to finally take me away.

I wished I had blacked out, but my own body seemed to want me to witness whatever horror was about to transpire. I didn't want to know why Anderson needed to crack open my chest. He'd taken so many organs out of my body, but it'd always been a kidney or bits of my liver. Never anything that I couldn't have lived without anyway.

But now Anderson bridged that gap between insanity and reality. He reached inside my chest and the burn radiated to my left side. His grip tightened and I sucked in a breath.

No. Surely he wouldn't go so far.

The thump of my heart strained against Anderson's grasp. He leaned in, squeezing as a tremor overtook my body. "Forgive me," he whispered.

My tongue rolled as I tried to speak. I

couldn't. The muse effects were too strong and the pain swept up and down my limbs like lightning.

Anderson closed his eyes and pulled my beating heart from my chest.

SUCCUBUS ON STEROIDS

Sonya

*N*ever before had I felt so powerful and yet at the same time, on the verge of losing control.

Emotion overpowered my senses, and at first I thought it was fear. The image of David's pale corpse blocked my vision and I shook my head, struggling to breathe. When I let the tears come I realized it wasn't fear constricting my throat, but the reality of my failure.

With a growl of frustration I ripped off my heels and tossed them into the road. Let them be destroyed, blasted things. My bare feet couldn't feel the pain of the jagged street as I broke into a run. I jerked my phone out of my pocket and took a sharp left to follow the bold green line. I didn't fail to notice my walking icon had been replaced with a bicycle. Stupid Google. Doesn't have a "Succubus on Steroids" setting.

Anderson was going to regret messing with me. I didn't care if he had something to block my powers. He couldn't block my fist. Even if he wasn't human, he wouldn't come back from a smashed-in skull.

After jogging for fifteen minutes, my breath still came slow and easy. My heart retaliated against my raging emotion and thumped with a steady beat. The power bubbled from my necklace and merged into my soul, giving me a bottomless source of energy. No matter how upset I was, my body wanted to act as if I was lounging on a beach basking in the sun.

The faster I ran, the more I realized I was bringing attention to myself. Cars slowed. Strangers walking on the street jerked to a halt to stare, men with lust and women with awe. Was I glowing? Maybe. But it didn't matter. I'd failed David. All this time I'd entertained the fantasy I could save him with a fully charged Blood Stone. My mother had told me of its regenerative powers. Although, she'd never spec-ified if those powers could be gifted to another. It was a faint hope I'd clung to in order to justify what I'd done to David. My selfishness was almost crippling. Why hadn't I just let myself die?

Tears evaporated off my cheeks and hoarse sobs scratched in my throat. My legs pumped and I pushed myself into a frantic run as my face scrunched in pain.

Why was I born this way? I shouldn't be on this planet, plaguing men with my poisonous kisses. Being an unfaithful girlfriend to Sarah, who only deserved the best. But it was too late for that now. My mother didn't drown me when I was born as I would have, had I been her. Instead she raised me with the knowledge of what I was. How cruel was she to teach me the difference between good and evil, when I was doomed to sin?

An ancient medical building loomed when I rounded the last bend and I snorted a laugh. Of course. The sign read:

Seattle Biological Research Center

I should have known. This place was the highest running rumor in Seattle for the creepy, haunted bio center that was all but shut down, yet still accepted cadavers and experimental medical patients, and the best possible place Anderson could hide. I'd been dared more than once to brave the mostly-abandoned research center at night, although the dare had always come from an infatuated stranger who wanted to flatten me against a dark wall. Little did they know the favor I did them by declining.

I drew in a deep breath and approached the building. This time not for fun, but for redemption. And as if to encourage why I was here, my necklace sizzled, as if sensing my need and dousing my body with energy. There was no doubt I was glowing now. My skin burned hot and glinted red off the lamp poles like tiny embers.

Four pristine cameras clashed against the medieval, mossy exterior of the research building. Their dark lenses stared at the abandoned parking lot with dead vulture eyes. I rolled my shoulders back and took three more steps. The cameras swirled onto my face and I thrust my middle finger in the air.

"Fuck you, Detective," I snarled. "I'm coming for you!"

SHE'S HERE

Luke

I was alive, which meant two things. One: Anderson hadn't been able to take my powers, even when activating them to peak performance. And two: I could fucking regenerate my own heart. Holy shit.

I crawled in the darkness towards a dull red light. Anderson was in the security room. That meant he was expecting someone.

"Luke? Is that you?" Sarah whispered.

I crawled to the bars and peered at her, letting my eyes adjust to the dim light. She had a nasty gash across her cheek and was bound to a chair. A strange hiss sounded every time she breathed. She wasn't doing so good.

She softened when she saw me. "You really are one of them." Her voice held marvel and awe.

One of what? What the fuck did that mean?

Sarah smiled, a friendly kind of smile that said everything was going to be okay, even if I didn't understand. The kind of smile my mother had given me right before she'd been taken off to prison.

"Luke," she pressed.

I pulled myself closer to the bars and rested my face against the cool metal, sticking my nose through the cell like a hound stuck inside a car.

"She'll be here soon. The one you're meant to protect."

I was so weary of this prophecy. Would this mystery girl really come into my life? How was I supposed to protect her? The second Anderson got ahold of that succubus and gained her soul-sucking ability, he'd be unstoppable.

Then I felt the boom. It was just as my mom's vision had described. Her presence would hit me and the need to protect her would overpower my senses.

The room remained dark but light flashed

across my vision like exploding stars. I scrambled to the back of the cell and fumbled against the loose stone, getting my hidden key.

It was time to get the fuck out of this God-forsaken place and save the world.

MYSTERY MAN

Sonya

The cameras followed me as I stomped to the front double doors. Expecting resistance, I pushed as hard as I could to break the hinges. Yet the doors weren't locked and flung across the room at my touch, crashing into a stack of chairs, reducing the pile to splinters. I couldn't help the grin that spread across my face. It was damn nice having real power for once.

The lobby looked just as I'd imagined it would, full of draped waiting chairs, minus the stack I'd destroyed, and an old reception desk covered in a thick layer of dust taking up the majority of the lobby in a wide arc. Cheap paintings lined the walls depicting research scientists nobody knew or cared about. I stepped inside and ignored the splinters crunching under my feet.

There wasn't a single light on in the place, not that it mattered. I glowed brighter than ever. The amulet around my neck burned hot and I gripped it for reassurance and strength. It was like holding a piece of red-hot coal, but one that fed me its warmth. Its stored power seeped into my hand and bled through my skin, muscles, and bone, empowering me like I'd never been strengthened before.

"Careful," said a voice from the loudspeaker. "Don't waste all your magic. I'll be needing it."

I jerked at the sound, but no one was in sight. The only sign of movement was a glistening camera straining against cobwebs as it followed my movements.

"Seriously?" I shouted. "You're going to talk to me from an intercom? Don't hide from me like a coward!"

"I'm not hiding." Detective Anderson's calm voice echoed through the room. "I'm documenting this moment for the judge." He snickered. "Thanks for glowing and removing all doubt of what you are."

I scoffed. "Even if I'm revealed to the humans, what kind of judge would side with you? What kind of justice system lets you go free and puts me behind bars?"

He laughed, and continued to laugh until the point of almost becoming hysterical. "Put you behind bars?" His voice went up a pitch as if I was being ridiculous. "Demons don't get put behind bars. They get sent back to hell."

I stomped towards the camera and growled. "I'm not a fucking demon! If anyone is a demon around here, it's you! You killed David!"

He chuckled, this time sounding as if he pitied me. "We both know you're at fault for his death, as you are for countless others. And now is a chance for your redemption. Come inside."

The camera swerved to the reception desk and a light blinked on from behind the fogged glass of the employee entrance.

I glared. "Why the hell would I go in there?"

Sarah's frantic voice burst through the intercom. "Sonya? Don't listen to him! Get the fuck out of here! He has—" Her words were cut short by a soft thump and muffled cry.

"Trade yourself for your girlfriend," said Detective Anderson, "or there'll be more blood on your hands."

My eyes went wide. "What's to tell me you won't kill her anyway? I'm not going to walk into some trap. Just let her go!"

He laughed and Sarah's whimpers lingered in the background, both from the intercom and some faint echo from behind the door. "What choice do you have?" said Detective Anderson. "Either enter into my care, and your girlfriend goes free, or cause trouble and I'll release my evidence to the government." His voice tinged with a sneer. "Every black-tied oaf will be after you then. The Black Widow in the flesh. Imagine what kind of reward there would be—"

The intercom released a rush of static before blipping off into silence. I crouched, waiting for the Detective to pounce from the shadows. But no movement came.

There was a crash from somewhere behind the door, sounding almost like it came from below ground. I straightened and stared at the fogged window, waiting for signs of life. What came next was a scream of rage. A man's scream, but it wasn't Detective Anderson's. The sound rolled through the hall and found its way into my chest and settled there like living thunder. I gripped my heart and cried out, not at any sort of pain but the shock of this feeling of invasion. What the heck was this? No... Who was this?

The scream was followed by the frantic slap of bare feet hitting the ground, and whoever it was, was heading straight for me.

Curling my fingers into fists, I prepared myself for whatever monster Detective Anderson had set loose. Perhaps this was his secret weapon, how he'd subdued my powers and Sarah's. Whatever it was, it sounded big.

The gorgeous naked man who burst from the employee's entrance was not at all what I'd expected and the undeniable connection of his magic hit me straight to the gut.

I balked. This... *man,* was one of the four? He held a piece of my heart and was a piece of my soul that would determine my destiny?

He stared at me, likewise taken aback as our connection sizzled through the air like fire. He was covered in dirt and blood, but that didn't diminish his exotic beauty. His wild eyes caught onto mine before lowering to the hidden rune astride my navel that sang for him.

I relaxed my shoulders. "Are you okay?"

I'm not sure why I asked such a silly question. There he was with his willy swinging away and his six-pack abs covered with nasty looking scabs and caked layers of dried blood. Whatever he'd been through, he was far from okay.

He just stood there and stared. His eyes were such a wild blue that I wanted to coax his gaze back to me.

Spreading my fingers and holding out my palms in what I hoped was a non-threatening motion, I slowly approached him. "You're safe now, okay?"

He cocked his head and peered into my face, but then he flinched when his eyes fell onto my amulet. Without warning he released a sound unlike any I'd ever heard from any human. His scream pummeled me from all directions and unseen splinters shoved into my brain. I cried out and felt that invasion of *him* once again, but this time the rage was directed at me. I crumpled to the ground, unprepared for the onslaught from someone who was supposed to be one of my four.

My amulet lit up like a firecracker and a shockwave bellowed through the hall. By the time I regained my composure and could stand, he was gone.

My hands drifted to my side and I stared at the wide open door. The only thing that moved me from my shock was one more scream... Sarah's.

I burst into the darkened hall of the employee basement. A wall of shit-scented air hit me in the face on my way down, but I didn't stop to gag. Sarah was still screaming.

"I'm coming!" I shouted. Her heart-wrenching wails wound my stomach into knots.

Stampeding down the dark staircase I bypassed a freakishly bloodied lab and continued my descent until I finally entered into a room with one bright bulb gleaming over my girlfriend bound to a chair, not by chains, but by fucking plastic zip ties. There were all kinds of odd para-phernalia filling the room, including grey jars with floating body parts and a small prison cell that reeked of feces, yet there was no Detective Anderson in sight. The only evidence he'd ever been here at all was a trail of blood leading to a cracked door at the end of the hall. The coward had escaped.

Sarah continued to scream as if she'd been

stabbed. Her eyes were squeezed shut and she shook her head, tossing her sagging blonde curls into her face and strained against the binds. It didn't make sense. A muse was strong enough to get out of that and even if the telling bloodstain at her chest suggested she'd actually been stabbed, she should have convinced her body to heal by now.

I rushed to her side and shook her by the shoulders. "Sarah! I'm here. Why are you screaming?"

Finally, she stopped thrashing and blinked. I expected her familiar striking blue eyes to greet me, the same color eyes that had attracted me to David. But just like David, dead, grey eyes stared back at me. It was as if Sarah's soul had been ripped out, leaving nothing but an empty husk that still breathed. "My God. What did that bastard do to you?"

Her lower lip trembled and tears streamed down her cheeks. "He took my powers!"

I froze, unable to register what she'd just said. Was such a thing even possible?

She sniffled and her gaze drifted to my neck-lace, still burning red-hot. "But it seems you've enough power for the both of us."

I clutched the Blood Stone, and even from its exuding, never-ending warmth I didn't think power was the fix for this. Sarah was human now.

Frowning, I rested my fingers on the plastic tie binding her wrist to the arm of the chair. It melted, and she yelped as her skin turned bright red. "Sorry," I whispered. She bit her lip and held still as I melted the other one.

Rubbing her wrists, she slumped and whimpered. I was accustomed to pain. I suffered through the ache of starvation on a regular basis, but Sarah was a muse. She wasn't used to it. What was she going through right now?

She whimpered, holding onto her chest and wheezing. "Can you... Is it possible to heal me?"

I'd never tried using my powers that way, but damn it, the Blood Stone had to be good for something. I pressed my palm against her chest and willed energy to go into her. It funneled without protest, seeming relieved to find an outlet in its ache to be used.

Sarah sucked in a breath and trembled. Her black eye turned pink and her breath lost its wheeze.

After a moment she seemed to compose

herself. She rolled her shoulders back and straightened. "Sonya," she whispered.

"Yes, are you all right?"

"I'm fine." Sarah ran her fingertips across the hollow of her chest. "That man. Did you see him?"

"What, the hot, naked one?"

She smirked. "Yeah, that's the one."

I shifted, resting on my knees. "What about him?"

She leaned in. "He can't die."

My heart skipped a beat. "What do you mean, he can't die?"

"I mean exactly what I say. I saw Anderson do things to him that should have killed a man. But whatever he cut out... it eventually grew back." She rubbed her wrists and stared into the dark depths of the cell. "I don't know how long he's been here, but I think it's been a long time. Anderson was trying to figure out how to take his powers, too. His gift of regeneration...immortality."

I wavered, unable to think of any supernatural who could regenerate, much less live forever. Even my kind had a limit to their lifespan. Sure, we could live for hundreds of years, but if you ripped out our heart it wouldn't grow back...

"Did Anderson keep him in there?" I asked, following Sarah's gaze to the iron bars.

Sarah nodded and drew in a deep breath before she continued, keeping her gaze on the cell floor. "His name's Luke. He had a key to his cell this whole time. He could have left whenever he wanted. I wasn't sure what he was waiting for until I touched him." She tilted her head and finally looked at me. "When you arrived in the lobby, he sniffed the air like a dog. He turned all frenzied, burst out of the cell and attacked Anderson. Bit him on the neck like some kind of maniac, and then ran upstairs." She looked me over head to toe. "You're who he's been waiting for."

"What do you mean, I'm who he's been waiting for?"

Sarah offered a weak smile. "You'll find out, I'm sure."

I rolled my necklace across my fingers, remembering Luke's bewilderment turning to fear. "I think this frightened him."

Shaking my head of thought, I stood, bringing myself back to my priorities. The mystery of the hot, naked man would have to wait. I'd saved Sarah, and now I needed to protect myself. "There's got to be a security station around here. Sounds like Anderson didn't have time to make off with the footage."

Sarah staggered to her feet and fell on my arm. She was so light and tiny, like a finch I could crush by accident if I wasn't careful.

She pointed to the end of the hall. "There. That's where he was before Luke scared him away."

Dragging Sarah along, we teetered our way to the door. Inside were two monitors showing the entrance hall and what must be the secondary exit Anderson had used to escape, but he didn't escape on his own. A stream of blood led to the curb before vanishing into a line of blackened tire streaks. He was long gone.

With a sigh I eased Sarah into a rickety green office chair and investigated the dusty equipment. There was only one box blinking a green light, and after a few button-jabs a tape popped out. Damn thing was ancient, but this meant there was only one recording in existence. I weighed the plastic in my hand before tossing it to the ground and grinding it under my naked heel. Detective Anderson just lost his evidence.

It was too hard to believe that this was all over. Was I safe? I looked back at Sarah and she shivered as if she couldn't get warm. No, it wasn't about me anymore. Maybe it never was. Detective Anderson was trying to figure out how to extract powers... He wasn't trying to stop me from murdering men. I scoffed. There was nothing honorable about his work.

Even though Sarah was the one who needed comforting, she knew me better than I knew myself and wobbled to my side. Without any concern for herself, she wrapped her arms around me. "You have to go after him," she whispered into my neck. My skin was hot and I knew it burned her to touch me, but she didn't pull away.

I stiffened. "What about you?"

She shrugged. "I'm human now. I can't be your girlfriend anymore."

I wrapped my arms around her body and hugged her tighter. "Sure you can."

She shook her head and pulled away, but I kept my hands bound behind her back. "No.

Even as a muse, I couldn't give you what you needed."

"How can you say that? I starved myself for you. I almost died. That's why David—"

She jerked out of my grasp. "I didn't ask you to starve."

Tears pricked at the edges of my eyes. "How else could I be faithful? By asking me to be exclusive, you were asking me to die. Even so, I tried..."

Pain and guilt warmed her pasty cheeks. "I thought you could feed off me. You acted like you could." Trails of wet tears streamed down her face again. "You *lied*."

Rage heated my chest and my skin sparked to life like a flame. Sarah stepped back when I thrust a finger in her face. "You don't know what it's like to love someone but never be able to be faithful. You should have known what it'd take." I pressed both hands against my chest. "I'm a succubus!"

Hurt spread across her features and no matter how angry I was, I knew I wasn't truly angry with her. As always, I blamed myself for ever being born.

"Sonya, I lied to myself too, okay? I let myself believe I was enough for you. But I wasn't."

"I'm sorry," I whispered, my rage evaporating. "I didn't mean to mislead you."

She smiled then, her features going soft. "Look. I understand now, okay? And that man, out there," she pointed to the door, "he's someone you're meant to be with. Before I lost my powers, I *felt* you inside of him, and now, I feel him inside of you." She grabbed my arm and her voice turned urgent. "Don't you know what that means? He's a part of your destiny. You need to go find him." Her fingers went lower, ghosting over my runes. "I didn't want your tattoos to mean anything. I avoided it as long as I could, just like I knew you couldn't feed off me. It's time I stopped lying to myself and face the truth. I'm not the one you're meant to be with, and that's okay."

I huffed a short laugh. "Seriously? And this guy you think is part of my destiny, or whatever, what do I have in common with him? He doesn't know me like you do."

Sarah flashed me a sad smile. "Maybe you have more in common than you think. You've both had your hearts ripped out." And then she walked out the door without looking back, leaving me alone with the glowing monitors. I clutched my chest that ached with pain that confirmed her words.

Sarah had ripped out my heart, and left me to bleed. I sure hoped she was right, and that man I'd met was one of my four, because the gift of his powers was the only way my heart would ever grow back.

PUBLIC TRANSPORT

Sonya

I'd saved Sarah and it didn't feel right to head to our cramped apartment and pretend nothing had happened. We were no longer together, no matter how much I wished it to be otherwise. There was a chasm between us and I couldn't even focus on it. An aching need pulled me in two different directions. I'd met two of the men who were part of my four, but there had to be some sort of mistake.

Zack was waiting for me when I returned to Derek's mansion. It should have startled me to find Sarah already in the living room drinking away her memories, which now that she was human, would be an effective means of treatment. But where else did she have to go? She needed help, and in Seattle, the Incubus King was where you found it.

Zack crossed his arms when he walked in. The tick in his jaw revealed he was relieved I'd come back, but he was still pissed off. "The King wants to talk to you two," he snapped, then promptly led me to what I could only describe as a throne room.

Derek lounged in a red velvet chair complete with spires and jewels. He wasn't just a king for show, but I knew this was a reminder of who I was... and who he was. I was just some random succubus he'd fucked, and now that he'd gotten what he wanted from me, he held my fate in his hands. The rune he'd activated on my ribcage was cold and silent. I slipped a hand under it and scratched at the smooth skin.

He might think he was done with me, but I wasn't done with him.

Derek motioned for Sarah to approach him. He would be gentle and polite with a muse in the room, especially given who Sarah's father was. One of three powerful male muses who held the fate of all supernaturals in their palms was a force to be reckoned with. "Tell me what has transpired, muse, and I will aid you with all the protection I have to offer."

She flinched at the term. He hadn't realized that she'd lost her powers. "Sonya thwarted a supernatural I haven't come across before." She paused, as if debating to offer up Detective Anderson's unique power, but then continued. Wise girl. Don't ever give the Incubus King everything he needed. "He was holding a prisoner," Sarah continued. "I want Sonya to find the fugitive that has fled and I will return to my father and seek out the perpetrator."

Derek rubbed his chin. "I see. Sounds like you have it all planned out. Well, I shall gladly offer my assistance. I have airlines and private jets—"

"I can take care of myself," Sarah said and propped a hand on her hip. She did that when she wanted everyone to think she was confident, but she was actually about to fall apart. I didn't know how she planned on getting to Miami, but she wasn't going to give Derek a chance to find out she'd lost her powers. "Give Sonya public transport," she added. She glanced at me as determination and rage glittered in her eyes. "He'll be heading to New York, so you best send her in the morning on the next flight out. We don't want her to draw attention. The supernatural is skittish, but I want Sonya to find him and bring him back to me as soon as possible."

I suppressed the growl that threatened to emanate from my throat. Public transport my ass. She just wanted to punish me.

"Very well," Derek said with a nod. He slipped his hand over the arm of the chair and leaned, the folds of his shirt opening to reveal the hard lines of his chest. His gaze met mine and he grinned. "I'll send two of my men to escort her, if that is permitted."

Sarah glanced back at me and my eyes widened. No. C'mon, Sarah, no. He just wants to capture me like a toy and he's going to send his goons to bring me kicking and screaming back to him.

"Very well," she agreed.

Damn it.

FIRST CLASS

Sonya

The strawberry daiquiri left a wet drizzle against my palms. The ice was nearly melted, but I couldn't bring myself to raise the drink to my lips. The cabin interior was sweltering and all I wanted to do was get out of this stuffy airplane filled with sweaty men who seemed to be incapable of anything but leering at me.

"Excuse me, Miss?"

Wearily, I peered at the fidgeting flight attendant. By the way her knuckles went white as she gripped the headrest, I guessed she'd been standing there for some time trying to get my attention.

She swallowed. "Would you like me to get you a new daiquiri?"

My fingers tightened around the drink. "No. I'm fine, thank you."

Her lashes lowered as she considered the slush once more. Her lips forced into a tight smile and she bobbed her head before heading back down the aisle.

This stupid drink was all I had left of Sarah. I was pissed off at her, but at the same time my heart ached. Thanks to the Blood Stone that had saved her, humans acted bizarre around me. Men openly stared and rolled their hips in their seats and I sighed dejectedly. I was a living ball of lust and I couldn't help how I made them feel. I didn't ask for this curse.

The women were even worse. I avoided their gazes as best I could. My powers never had an effect on women before, but now it seemed I'd changed. I caught them staring just as much as the men, if not more. Often their gazes lowered to my chest. My leather jacket plumped with my breasts and my pendant resting on my bosom. The Blood Stone was quiet, but constantly warped the air around me like a sexual force-field. I exuded with its power. It hadn't been phased by the juice I'd taken from it to heal Sarah from a bullet wound.

A jab in my ribs made me jolt and my drink toppled over my tray. Pink slush splattered in all directions and I cursed, turning to investigate the source of the disturbance, only to find a small boy pushing his nose between the seats like a hound.

"Jeffrey!" his mother cried. "I'm so sorry. I don't know what's gotten into him." She peeled the boy away from the seat and offered me an apologetic smile paired with a blush.

The attractive flight attendant reappeared with cocktail napkins and began dabbing away at the mess. The useless bits of paper greedily sucked up the slush and only served to smear the sticky ice across the plastic. She kept her fretting over the tray and didn't use the excuse to clean my jacket and cop a feel, which I found odd.

"Penny!" An elderly man with slicked-back grey hair and the biggest Adam's apple I'd ever seen pushed her aside. "Allow me to take care of this."

Penny frowned down at the sad little napkins and moved out of his way.

The man smiled and wiped the slush into a bucket. "I'm terribly sorry for this, Miss. Please, let's get you out of this seat. We have an opening in first-class. Please relocate to the front as our apology."

I balked. I'd gotten a cabin ticket for a reason. If I'd wanted first-class I could have simply asked for one. Heck. If I wanted this man's kidney he'd cut it out right now if I told him it'd make me happy.

But as I stared into his eyes, I saw a flicker of concern. I'd expected knee-buckling lust, which is all I'd ever gotten from men as of late. But this one seemed unaffected. I squinted, trying to make out any supernatural features. Aside from the piercing blue eyes, he seemed unremarkable. His friendly face was framed by kempt white hair, and his outstretched hand, waiting to guide me to my upgraded seat, was accented by wrinkles. An incubus didn't age, so that meant he was something I didn't understand. I frowned. I didn't like not understanding anything.

I pressed my lips together and squirmed out of my chair, trying to avoid the trickling pink droplets. The elderly man trailed behind me as I picked my way through the narrow aisle to the front of the plane, passing through multiple drapes as I escalated through economy and business class until I reached the front hatch where I'd entered. I glanced at it before considering the over-exuberant drape running past it, shimmering with different shades of blue as it moved with the subtle rolling of the plane that would take me to first class.

I peered over my shoulder and the elderly man smiled warmly and nodded. "Your new seat is 2B."

I swallowed hard. That was really their only seat left? That was right across from...

With a sigh, I broke through the fragile curtain, sending the metal rings clanging against the rail. A few passengers turned to glare at such a rude intrusion, until they saw who had entered. Even without the Blood Stone, I was my mother's daughter and could command a room with ease. Or in this case, a class. But with the Blood Stone, my power seeped through my skin and wafted over the crowd like noxious gas. Shoulders rolled back, backs straightened, and all eyes locked onto me.

All eyes...except for the guy sitting in 2A.

Nate, one of the many sons of the Incubus King, and my unwanted escort, took a long swig of his whiskey before exhaling with satisfaction and swirled the gold-tinted ice in his glass. I frowned, not because he was pretending not to notice I'd been forced into first-class, but because he drank whiskey like I did. Why'd he have to ruin a good thing with that smirk?

Finally, he acted surprised to have realized I was standing there while everyone continued to stare at me. He smiled his obnoxious, boyish smile and I returned his unspoken gloat with a glare.

Without a word, I stomped to my seat and plopped down with as little grace as I could muster, crossed my arms, and set my mouth into a pout.

"What's wrong, babe? Do I get under your skin?" he asked with a wicked grin that matched his father's, except I'd been fighting the fact that Nate stirred the prophecy within me. He didn't know that a rune across my stomach burned with need every time he was around, screaming at me that this insufferable human was one of my four... no. No fucking way was I going to accept that.

I glared at Nate, and then transferred my rage to the elderly flight attendant who seemed to be quite pleased with himself.

I crossed my arms. "Don't tell me you got that little boy to poke me?"

The old man bowed and offered me a cup of ice water in a much nicer cup than what I'd received in economy. "Dear me, no," he said. "I can't control children any more than I can control anyone else." His eyes crinkled in another smile, this time hinting at some hidden joke I didn't get, before he shuffled to the back of the cabin and disappeared behind the curtain.

An exasperated sigh escaped my throat as I jerked down my armrest and glared at the unnecessarily large cup holder which had some-thing still inside. I fished out a wadded piece of paper. Well-written calligraphy swirled through the scented paper with my name on it. Inside, the note anonymously invited me to dinner, followed by an address which I knew far too well. Ever since I'd inherited the d'Ange mansion, my grandmother's, then my mother's, and now mine. The handwriting suggested someone in my family was still here, but who? Dammit, I had to find out now.

This sucked. Just because I was going to New York didn't mean I had any intention of revisiting my inherited home. If I went there, I'd have to finally admit my mother was dead and I was ready to move on. I wasn't.

I glanced at Nate and he shrugged before turning back to his tablet and pulled a black headset over his tousled hair.

With a growl I crumpled the note and shoved it into my pocket. Dammit. My plan had been to go straight to Queens and look for Luke. Luke, the only reason I hadn't split in two when Sarah left my life for good. Luke... one of my supernatural four who deserved a place in my soul.

I gagged on the thought. How pathetic was I? Maybe going to a party in my own house would be a good idea. I glanced again at Nate, trying to see him as his father had asked me to. *A needed distraction until you find what you're looking for.*

He was hot, there was no doubt about that. But he was constantly joking and acting like he was twelve. Hardly my definition of sexy. But at this very moment he seemed almost serious as he focused on the movie playing on his tablet. His jaw went firm and his amber eyes remained steady on the screen until they flashed at me and I drew in a quick breath before looking away.

Maybe this wouldn't be so bad after all.

*N*ate didn't say a word when the elderly flight attendant followed us from the gate and crammed into the mid-sized elevator with us and twenty other people.

To my surprise, both the flight attendant and Nate positioned themselves as a barrier between me and the elevator's jittery passengers. Given that I literally oozed sexual energy, it was a much-needed precaution. Though the humans couldn't see it, a soft red glow hissed off my skin like steam and tickled their noses. They would twitch and flick their eyes, unaware of what was bothering them.

Three men closest to me started to arch their necks, trying to peer over my guardian's broad frames. The flight attendant sputtered a wet cough, driving the men back in disgust. He politely covered his mouth and excused his outburst while Nate wedged himself even closer to me.

I became acutely aware of Nate's body pressing against my chest. His warmth radiated through our clothes and joined with the ever-present radiance of my Blood Stone resting on my bosom. It felt right, somehow, even though it shouldn't have. Nate was one of the King's sons, and not Luke. Not the man Sarah had said was my soulmate and "reason to be." I shook my head. Both men sounded like a ridiculous fit for me.

Then I realized what felt so different about this moment. Nate wasn't his jolly, bad-jokes self. When the other passengers leered my way, his body would go rigid and he crossed his arms, trying to make himself as big as possible like a peacock. His head swiveled side-to-side, inspecting the crowded elevator for any sign of danger.

Likewise, the flight attendant set his jaw and widened his stance, as if he was readying himself to spring into action.

In spite of his age, the old man's broad shoulders and even wider forearms assured he was stronger than he seemed at first glance.

My hand rose to my chest, subconsciously pressing against the lump that was my locket resting underneath the leather, searching for comfort and strength. If I was in danger, I could protect myself.

The elevator released a loud screech and my skin went white-hot with fear. Sure, I could protect myself from a lust-crazed human, but I couldn't stop an elevator if it decided to go into free-fall.

The lights flickered and between the moments of illumination and darkness, I jolted upright and my chest went tight with fear. There, a woman in the very back, had her eyes locked on me and didn't seem the least bit concerned about the jerky up-and-down of the elevator. Instead, she waited for me to notice her gaze, and then she smiled, and *vanished.*

WELCOME HOME

Sonya

"*D*id you see that?" I hissed into Nate's ear.

The only indication that Nate had heard me was the slight twitch of his gaze. But he remained fixated, scanning the elevator for the threat.

Although what he could possibly do if we were in danger, I had no clue. How could we protect ourselves from a woman who could vanish into thin air?

I unzipped my jacket and let my naked hand scramble through the fabric to take the Blood Stone in a solid grip. The heat against my fingertips was soothing, but for some reason, it didn't feel like it was enough.

The passengers murmured and fidgeted, casting wary glances in my direction as the lights dimmed and the elevator screeched to a halt on the ground floor.

The second the doors opened, Nate took my wrist as if I were a child who he might lose at any moment and jerked me outside. I suppressed a yelp, but didn't resist. Whatever was going on was way above my pay grade.

Nate continued to drag me along and I tripped at his heels while the elderly flight attendant silently followed. In a moment of wistfulness, I'd hoped we'd stop to get our suitcases, but Nate sped right on by the carousel with the bright blue numbers flashing our flight number and jerked me outside. Whatever had them so spooked, we couldn't stick around, especially not for my suitcase filled with my favorite heels and sad little mementos of Sarah which mainly consisted of strawberry daiquiri shakers.

Nate sped over the crosswalk and into the parking garage, only stopping when we arrived at what was apparently our ride. I stared at it. Really? A Chevy? One of the mighty incubus princes, human as he may be, wouldn't be caught dead in such a piece of junk.

To my surprise, Nate shoved me into the backseat like a piece of baggage and nodded to the flight attendant to take the driver's seat. Nate slipped in beside me and continued to scan through the windows as if he was a guard dog on high alert.

When the car gurgled to life and we puttered out of the terminal entrance way, everyone seemed to relax.

"Would someone mind telling me what the hell is going on?" I blurted.

The car jostled over a speed bump and Nate cast me an apologetic glance. "I'm not sure how she found us." He looked at his hands curling into fists in his lap. "You're not supposed to know about her."

I narrowed my eyes. "About who?"

He drew in a deep breath, held it as if whatever he was about to say was difficult to admit, and then expelled it with the words, "Your daughter."

I balked. A hundred thoughts flew through my mind, but none of them helped that statement make any sense. I'd never given birth, and if I did, I'd certainly remember it. "What the hell are you talking about?"

The flight attendant caught my wild gaze in the rearview mirror. Towering buildings cast us into a shadow, blocking out what little light the overcast skies offered. "There's a reason I look so old," he said. His eyes went hard and a flash of anger crossed his face. Then it transformed into resignation and he looked back to the street. "The price for your Blood Stone wasn't just a night with the King. You affected others, too."

I blinked, my chest constricting and my breath coming in short gasps. My eyes followed the wrinkled lines on his face. "What do you mean?"

Nate waved a hand dismissively. "You'll learn about it soon enough. For now, know that when you slept with my father and mother," he said with a surprisingly straight face, "you helped them create something they've been after for a very long time."

Something. Not someone, but something.

I knew that I had helped Silvia and Derek conceive, but that had been barely a few days ago. And last I'd checked, it took nine months to have a baby, and the girl we saw in the elevator had to have been at least sixteen.

"But—" I began, but Nate cut me off.

"It's not a *natural* birth, by any means. You are her mother, just as much as Silvia is."

Whoa. That was far too much to take in. I shook my head and groaned, leaning into the cigarette-scented seat.

The car eased to a stop and waited at one of the many traffic lights. There seemed to be a new light every two feet. I gazed out the window, hoping to be calmed by the sight of a tree or friendly face, but all I saw was a blinding sea of yellow paint. We were surrounded by an incessant number of taxis and I numbly wondered why they couldn't use a more attractive color.

"We'll make it on time," the flight attendant announced.

I shifted in the seat and peered over his shoulder, trying to match his gaze in the rearview mirror. "On time for what?"

He grinned as the arrow turned green and he rounded the corner, revealing a mansion in the middle of Manhattan. It towered over the street and I'd completely forgotten the bronzed statues decorating each pillar, each boasting stone women dancing around the edges of the roof, holding only bits of cloth and leaves to cover their bodies. Their grey eyes peered down at the street and glittered with joy as if they could see me. I scanned the clouds for rain, but couldn't see a drop.

Nate nudged me with his elbow. "Welcome home."

A DISTRACTION

Sonya

The second I walked inside the d'Ange mansion, I was hit by the scent of lilac potpourri. It was so much like my grandmother's perfume. I couldn't help but draw in a deep breath and let my memory spiral back to when she would greet me in the doorway and I'd run into her arms, wrap my legs around her waist and my tiny arms around her neck.

When I opened my eyes, my memory had become flesh. My grandmother stood in all her glory, even though she was well into her six-hundreds, she boasted the body of a twenty-year-old and a skimpy silk dress with a floral pattern complete with a slit running up her thigh. She smiled and spread her arms wide. "My Sonya," she purred with her familiar British accent.

Tears filled my eyes as I realized I somehow wasn't hallucinating, and my grandmother hadn't tragically died in the fire that killed her and my mother six years ago. My breath hitched. If my grandmother was alive, did that mean my mother had made it out too?

I staggered towards her and resisted the urge to fling myself into her arms as if I were a child again. Yet, when I saw her same healthy blush and her nonchalant smile, anger bloomed and found its way to my fists, curling them into balls as my shocked cry turned into a snarl. "Where have you been?" I hissed. "All these years, I thought you were dead!" My voice went shrill and my vision blurred with salty tears.

My grandmother's face softened and an array of regret and pain swept across her features. "I'm sorry," was all she said.

Nate rested a warm hand on my shoulder. I snatched away from his touch. "Where's mother?" I demanded. The impossible hope choked the breath from my throat and I staggered, waiting for an answer.

My grandmother crossed her arms over her chest as if to protect herself from the anger rolling off my skin. Because of the Blood Stone, my rage was a tangible thing sending waves of heat billowing through the room.

"Her death wasn't a lie," she whispered. "Please, Sonya." Her lips tugged into a forced smile. "Come inside. We've made a welcome party for you." Her smile widened, gaining confidence. "We should celebrate our reunion, my Sonya." When I didn't respond, she added, "It's what your mother would have wanted."

Jazz music lingered in the background and glasses clinked together like rain droplets hitting a tin roof. But I couldn't celebrate, not when the hope of my mother's survival dangled in the air, only to be snatched away again. "No," I said.

My grandmother pinched her eyebrows together and opened her mouth to speak. But I didn't want to hear her excuses. She'd lied to me and let me believe I was alone for six years. She didn't deserve a chance to explain herself. "Enough," I snapped. "I'm not joining your stupid party. In fact, I'm not going to be staying very long." Without a moment's hesitation, I rushed past her and resisted the magnetic pull of her lilac perfume. It sent comfort and warmth tingling through my chest.

Thankfully, the scent faded as I rounded a corner and stomped down the hall. Nate's soft footsteps followed and I didn't protest. I didn't really want to be alone, I just didn't want to face my grandmother. Not now, not like this.

When I didn't snap at him to leave, Nate quickened his pace so that he was only one step behind. I led us to the only place I knew to go: the library.

Once inside, the tightness binding my chest loosened and I could finally draw in a deep breath. The rows of ancient oak shelves housed hundreds of books and towered all the way to the ceiling. Cathedral arches with glossy, dark wood accented the trove of musty treasures and I couldn't help but smile. I took off my heels and let my toes curl in the softness of the plush rugs, heirlooms from Persia.

"Nice racks," Nate said, breaking the comforting silence with a crude joke.

I cast him a mournful look. "Really, Nate. Not now."

He quirked a smile. "Just trying to lighten the mood."

I rolled my eyes, but appreciated his effort. In spite of myself, I felt better already.

As I ran my hands across the shelves, drawing comfort from the long-seeded memories of my early childhood, Nate followed like a shadow. "So," he whispered, his voice sounding huskier and sexier than usual. "Why are you so interested in finding this man you know so little about?"

My heart skipped a beat. "My so-called-dead grandmother comes back to life after six years, and you want to know about Luke?" It made sense. Even if Nate couldn't feel it, if he was really one of my four, he was bound to Luke too.

He chuckled. "I'm not looking to dredge up family drama. But I *would* like to know why you've come to New York."

I could have told him to go screw himself, that it was none of his business, but the honest curiosity in his voice only made me want to open up. "Luke and I are connected," I said. "Sarah told me I should find him, and when I lost her, it felt like she'd died. It felt like...that was her last wish." I left out the part where my rune stopped responding to her. Whatever connection her and

I had was now severed. It was time for me to find my four, but I wasn't sure if I was ready.

He scoffed and irritation prickled down my spine. "She didn't die," he pressed. "She lost her powers. That's all."

"You're human; what would you know of it?" I closed my eyes and leaned my cheek against the shelves for strength. "Becoming human is just as good as dead for a muse."

He sighed and came dangerously close. Just when I thought this was another joke, his warmth encased my body and he ran his nails over my arms, sending goosebumps over my skin ending with his fingers lacing over my knuckles. "And what do you think will happen when you find your mystery man?" His voice was a challenging whisper, daring me to say this was anything but a foolish errand. "What will you do then?"

What *would* I do? I'd hope for the impossible, that's what. I'd hope that this damn prophecy was true. That Luke was a piece of my soul and could absolve me of my guilt and torment. Only true love could redeem someone like me, and how desperately I longed for absolution.

Nate's whisper sent shivers through my body.

"I can't pretend to know what it's like to be a succubus," he said, "but I think what you need is to stop being so hard on yourself."

I shivered, unable to turn and look at him. Ignoring the growing tension, I shrugged him off and plucked a book from the shelf, pretending to be fascinated, even though I couldn't force myself to read a single word. I went stiff when Nate's warm hand fell on my shoulder.

"I don't need to feed," I said. "And even though you might think I'm worth it, I assure you, I'm not worth dying for."

He wrapped an arm over my collarbone, letting his fingers drape across my breasts and caress the Blood Stone. "That's why this is such a special opportunity. You can enjoy what I have to offer without damning me to death, all because of this delightful, red gem."

I blinked and peered up into his face. He smiled, and it wasn't that boyish smile to which I'd grown so accustomed, but the confident smile with perfect lines that could only come from being a son of the Incubus King.

"I hadn't considered that possibility," I admitted.

His finger ran up my throat and traced my lips. "Not even once?"

My lips parted of their own accord as his breath on my face sent goosebumps spreading across my arms. He tested my neck with his teeth and instead of pulling away, a delicate moan escaped my throat.

His tongue found my earlobe and then he whispered, "I may be human on the outside, but there are supernatural qualities I still inherit from my father."

My eyes grew with curiosity and a yearning inside of me responded to his promises. I pulled away, only to be secretly delighted when he grabbed my waist and forced me close. His stiff erection pressed into my hip and my breath hitched with anticipation.

Growling with victory, he laced his fingers through mine before taking me with a hungry kiss. The sweet taste of his tongue sent chills through my chest and made me yearn for more than just his mouth.

Then, at the worst possible moment, Luke's face popped into my mind. I jerked away from Nate and the lust in the air turned cold.

"What is it?" he whispered. His eyes glazed

over with concern, but as he searched my face, he smirked. "You're thinking about Luke, aren't you?"

I expected him to be hurt, or perhaps jealous, instead he seemed to relax. "What is it?" I asked.

He grinned. "There's something... I don't know. This is going to sound weird, but it feels like it makes sense. I mean, you're a succubus. You're not supposed to be with just one guy." He shrugged. "Maybe I'm okay with sharing, as long as you can handle me when it's my turn."

While I was distracted by his honesty, his mouth ravished mine with new vigor and I squeaked in surprise. "No, Nate I—" My words were cut short as he thrust his hand down my pants and sent a surge of pleasure through every nerve ending as his fingers thrust inside. I should have resisted, but my disloyal body bucked underneath him and wanted more. The rune that responded to him, just astride my navel, burned with hot need. He was one of my four, one of my men that would fulfill my every need.

I closed my eyes, giving into the waves of hot bliss running through my insides. Nate gave a husky growl against my neck, sensing my acceptance, before sinking his teeth into my skin again, this time harder than before. The flash of pain was a delightful contrast to the pleasure and mixed its sweet tones in my body.

I hadn't even touched him, but the taste of his arousal wafted against my senses. My instinct screamed to drink it in, but instead, I redirected my focus and drew on the power of my Blood Stone. It ignited under my command, sending a bright flash and warm glow wafting through the room. My own cry of victory shuddered on my breath as I delighted in the assurance that I could have this, I could have him, without consequences. Without regret.

Nate ripped off my pants and pummeled me into the row of shelves and I grappled my fingers behind me for a handhold. Books toppled out of their organized piles and tumbled to the ground as Nate lifted me off my feet. I wrapped my legs around his hips and realized how badly I wanted a guilt-free night with someone who only wanted to take all my cares away.

He didn't hesitate. The elastic of my already thin thong broke as he clawed it aside. Likewise, I fumbled at his jeans and was delighted to see they were already unbuttoned. One pull on the zipper and his thick erection made a brief appearance before disappearing between my thighs. The supple skin found its target and thrust inside. I arched my back and hit my head against a shelf, but the pleasure slamming through me dwarfed the pain. Nate's desperate thrusts pummeled into me and didn't stop; it was as if he needed me right now as much as I needed him. Even when the pleasure spiked and I couldn't hold my orgasm any longer, and I quivered and contracted hard around him, he didn't cease. He kept going and flashed me a pleased grin at my shocked face, as if this was just the start. His mouth found mine and he continued to pound into me as he muffled my cries with his tongue.

A memory of his father taking my orgasms with ease streaked through my mind and I realized this is what he'd meant. His heritage. He could fuck me as long as he wanted, make me orgasm until I was screaming, and not even break a sweat.

He was definitely one of my four.

His lips broke away from mine as he watched my face, seeming to enjoy the expression of ecstasy and shock I couldn't control.

I hung onto him for dear life with one hand,

and brought the other to my mouth for a firm bite. I'd already hit my climax three times, and he showed no signs of slowing. A deep ache I'd never felt before burned in my stomach and threatened to overwhelm me. I bit down harder and hoped I could muffle my own screams.

"Tonight, you're mine," he whispered confidently as he pulled my hand from my mouth. "Tell me that you're mine."

When I didn't respond, he slowed his thrusts to a soft in-and-out, giving me blessed relief, but keeping me on the edge of another cliff.

My lips parted and I realized it was true. In this moment, I'd do anything he wanted. "I'm yours," I breathed. The rune across my stomach hummed in approval.

He grinned and ran his fingers through the roots of my hair, just enough to get a good fistful before gripping and exposing my neck as I arched into the pull. He knew how to grab me without hurting me, and that just turned me on more.

"How do I make you feel?" he asked.

I closed my eyes and focused on the soft gyrating of his hips. My insides were so swollen and my wetness ran down the arch of my butt.

Thankfully to be absorbed by my shirt instead of my poor grandmother's book collection.

"You overwhelm me," I admitted.

I forced my eyes open to blink at him through the red haze of my Blood Stone's power, and basked in his stamina. I didn't have to explain that as a succubus, men didn't last long with me. This was an entirely new experience.

He slowed his movements even more, just barely moving and forcing me to push my own hips to keep the sensation of his lust going. I'd never been pushed this far, and I didn't want it to stop.

His tongue slid across my neck until it reached my earlobe. Chills ran over my arms as it briefly went inside my ear canal. "Do you want me to keep going?" he asked.

Words were beyond me now. I gripped the shelves and pressed my thighs against his hips as I lifted myself up and down on his crotch. A pathetic whimper came out when I couldn't replicate the intense thrust he'd been doing to me a moment before.

He smoothed my hair and forced me to look into his eyes. "I want to hear you beg."

The bastard. But I wanted him, so I parted my

lips and forced the words out. "Please," I whispered.

Nate leaned in closer, running his hand to the arch of my back and pulling me into his hard chest. "What was that?"

"Fuck me as hard as you can," I pleaded. "Fuck my brains out."

He smiled. "Yes," he said. "You understand now, poor succubus. You've always been the seductress. You've always melted men and given them what they needed so you could have your small bit of nourishment." He tilted his head sympathetically and pulled me up far too effortlessly. "But what have you ever gotten other than survival? What about overwhelming pleasure? What about being *taken*? Don't you want that?"

My eyes searched his, pleading for him to give me everything he'd just said. "Yes." I wrapped my fingers around his neck and hovered my lips over his. "Please, take me."

An evil smile spread across his face as he lowered me to the floor. I trembled as he pulled off my shirt, stopping only for a moment to rake his gaze over my runes. His eyes widened when he spotted his, the one that resonated with his own sexual energy he'd drilled into me. He reached out and grazed it with a gentle touch, making me shiver. "What is that?" he asked.

I smiled. "That... is a long story."

We didn't have time for long stories. Both of us panted with need and he twisted me onto all fours.

Nate thrust into me without warning and my insides exploded with the force. I cried out and didn't care anymore if someone heard. I'm a succubus. I have sex. My grandmother and her guests shouldn't be surprised, right?

Nate grabbed onto my hips and I knew I was in for the night of my life. He pounded, going faster and faster as the slapping of my ass against his thighs told me I was going to be either raw or bruised by the time he was done with me. Each thrust sent a cry of agonized pleasure shuddering through me as I clawed my fingers through the plush carpet.

Then he leaned over my body and groped his fingers across my flat stomach, running across the runes before settling onto the one that pulsed with his heat, then instead of going for my breasts, his fingers ran down until they reached my clit. He circled the swollen flesh, sending flurries of fresh pleasure through me as he continued to move his hips, but gently, letting me savor the graze of his touch.

"Delicious," he whispered into my ear. "I want a taste."

To my shock, he pulled out and rolled me on my back, his kisses following the same path his fingers had taken until his tongue found my swollen folds. It felt so good it hurt, and I cried out when he kissed and rolled his tongue across my flesh.

I tried to squirm away, embarrassed by how engorged I was. So much raw pleasure, so much blood all in one place, it was unfathomable that he would find it attractive.

His hands latched onto my hips and kept me where I was. I was drained and unable to fend him off, and instead let my head fall to the carpet in defeat. I gripped my Blood Stone for strength, drawing in the power to help me survive this pleasure. He was so turned on by me; I could feel it lingering in the air and plucking at me like short electric sparks. But what amazed me most was how much sexual energy *I* was exuding. My necklace drank it up and fed it back into my core, as if repulsed I would waste it into the air.

Heat ran through my skin and when I saw the

room was beginning to take on a blue hue, I looked down to Nate doing unimaginable things with his tongue. His eyes softly glowed with sexual energy, azure, like his father's, and it swarmed in his gaze as he pushed me to climax. It was so hot, to see him watching me while I exploded in his mouth.

He wiped his chin and grinned, satisfied with his handiwork. I, on the other hand, heaved, barely able to hold my head up.

"You're even more delicious than I imagined," he whispered as he drew himself over me. Gently, he pressed his erection into me, being careful not to overstimulate my impossibly swollen pussy.

He didn't look away as he gyrated. As his features softened I knew he was allowing himself to come to climax. It felt so intimate, far more than a fling with what was only meant to be a distraction. I couldn't pull myself away as he began to moan, the sound such amazing music to my ears. I felt so grateful for everything he'd given me that it made my heart pound to hear his pleasure. I latched onto his biceps and squeezed myself around his cock, hoping to strengthen his orgasm. I wasn't sure if I'd feel his ejaculation, everything was so hot already. But as he sped up, I knew there could be no doubt. I'd feel this one.

His eyes fluttered closed in bliss as he reached his climax. The veins on his neck bulged and heat exploded through my insides. I couldn't help but climax with him, the sensation and mere sight of him driving me to new heights of pleasure.

When the moment ended, I knew everything had changed. I wanted what I'd said in lust-drunkenness to be true. I wanted to be his. Not just tonight. For good.

*F*ucking Sonya had been a job, but after I'd done the deed, damn, she was more than a job to me. She'd unhinged something in me and I wasn't sure how much of it I could handle. As the son of an incubus, I could have sex as long as I wanted, control my orgasms with precision. Sonya was a new challenge, a succubus used to being the seductress. To see her vulnerable and the *need* in her eyes had made me feel something I'd never felt before. Not to mention, what was that damned rune? The moment I'd touched it… something in me had locked into place.

"And, what have you learned?" my father pressed, impatient to hear more of the triumph.

"Look, she's vulnerable right now," I snapped. "I don't want to do this anymore. Send someone else."

My father's deep chuckles filled my ears and I had the urge to jerk out the earbuds attached to my cell phone. But I needed him to agree with this. I had to get him to understand that I wasn't the right guy to find out Sonya's secrets... even though I was already too close to uncovering them all.

"Nathaniel," my father purred with mock concern, "is that guilt I hear in your voice? Or satisfaction?" He gave a soft mock-gasp. "Both?"

The moonlight trickled in my window and I stared at the motes dancing in the streak of light. "Send. Someone. *Else*," I said through gritted teeth.

"Look, son. You have a job to do, and you're going to put your sister above your unfortunate human conscience. Find out if Luke is what we think he is, and then we'll go from there. Got it?"

Right, Luke. He was another one, someone like me bound to Sonya and a power that was something so much greater than the Incubus King's plans for this world. I softly hit the back of my head against the wall in frustration. *No.*

"Sonya will understand," he continued. "This is for her best interest as well, you see? She'll be grateful when this is all said and done. If you care about her, you'll do as I say."

"Are you serious?" I said, not listening to the tiny voice in my mind screaming at me to shut up. Reminding me that my father was not *just* my father, but the most ancient Incubus on the planet and the King of a race I could never inherit. In his society, he didn't have to recognize me as his son. He could have just as easily killed me at birth rather than honor me with tasks, much less the task of seducing a succubus like Sonya.

"Tell me, son. What did one good fuck with her do to give you such ideas?" His voice turned mocking once again. "Did she laugh at you? Oh, is it better than that? Right when things were getting good, did she scream my name?"

I suppressed the growl rolling in the back of my throat and took a deep breath. It hadn't bothered me that he'd fucked Sonya first. But now, damn, it got under my skin. I didn't mind sharing her with men who deserved her, but my unholy father was not one of them. "Hardly," I said, trying to sound nonchalant. "I just—" I clenched my fists and squelched the tiny voice that was now shrieking like its life depended on it.

I knew I'd given Sonya the night of her life. I'd seen it in her eyes. That surprised me, knowing my father was literally the king of sex. I was human, and even if my Incubus heritage did wonders for my dick, there was no way I could have been the same. Realization wafted over me that for Sonya, she wasn't just turned on by a good lay. She'd felt my desire for her, my genuine concern. That's what she wanted, and there's no way in hell my father could ever have given her that.

I cleared my throat and tried to give my father something close enough to the truth to get him off my back. "I just don't want Sonya to get hurt."

"Touching," my father said. "Why don't you get some sleep and we'll talk about this when your head's screwed on straight. One of them, at least."

I gave one glance to the doorway, waiting any moment for Sonya to step through. I could feel her down the hall just three rooms away. I'd tasted her and her Blood Stone connected me to her desires, and right now, all she could think about was me. My dick got hard just thinking about it. With a blush, I realized my father was still on the phone. "Sure, *dad*," I said, making sure to emphasize in no way did I feel he deserved the title 'dad.' "Sleep sounds like a good idea."

The call ended with a click and a fluttering heartbeat approached me through the halls. I held my breath, waiting for the door to open, and to my surprise, it did. Sonya basked in the moonlight, already peeling away her silk robe. Her skin beckoned me, moist with her desire and her tongue flashing across her lips.

No way was I getting any sleep tonight.

THE DYING BLOOD STONE

Sonya

Waking up next to Nate was the best sight I'd had in many-a-morning. His naked chest gently heaved as he drew in deep breaths. I curled into his embrace, taking comfort in the strong, steady beat of his heart. It was different than when I'd awoken to his father and mother, and a part of me felt guilty to even be thinking of that now. But when I got past the perversion of it, I had to admit this was so much better. Nate had emotion and passion. My night with his father had only been lust and a touch of desperation.

I traced the arch of his nose, so like Silvia's,

and drew a line down his solid jaw, a perfect resemblance of his father. His features held the best of his parents, and yet, as he drew his eyes open and sleepily blinked at me, I realized he was something they weren't. Was that his humanity?

His gaze held such softness I'd never noticed in him before. He was always turning things into a joke, never taking me seriously, and seeming to generally be a giant pain in the ass. But now, as I matched his gaze with an affectionate smile, I realized he hid behind those jokes because his father didn't approve of his humanity. How sad, to have to always hide who you were. I could relate.

"Good morning," he breathed. Then he slid his thumb across my cheek. "You shouldn't sleep with makeup on. I thought you were a clown for a second."

I glowered and pulled out of his grasp. Way to destroy the moment. "I'll get washed up," I mumbled, keeping the sheets tight to my body and taking them with me to the bathroom. Nate's chuckles followed me like gnats and I slammed the door to keep them out.

Sunlight streamed in through the glazed window and sent the luxurious features of the oversized bathroom into a scene of stark reality. The light revealed the stains from standing water across the delicate marble countertops, specks of ingrained dirt in the tile's grout, and my own makeup-streaked face staring back at me in the fogless mirror.

"What you lookin' at?" I snapped at my reflection and frowned. I snatched a pristine towel and began scrubbing my face.

"What was that, babe?" Nate's muffled voice sounded from the other side of the door.

I rolled my eyes. "Nothing!"

When the skin under my eyes retained the dark hue from my makeup, I lathered the damp towel with soap and went at it again. What was I thinking getting so close to Nate? Was I really that fucking desperate?

I sighed and drew back the stained towel, successful in my mission to scrub my skin raw. Fresh pink glittered at me in the mirror and a small wave of satisfaction warmed my chest. Then I looked down to my necklace. The Blood Stone's power swirled, but seemed different than before. I grabbed it and yanked the chain over my neck to get a better look. I popped the locket open and gasped.

The stone had turned blue.

"What the fuck is this?" I demanded as I burst out of the bathroom.

I hadn't bothered to put on a robe that was hanging on the back of the door and instead of answering, Nate smirked and eyed my naked body. "Looks like somebody wants seconds," he tilted his head. "Or to be more accurate, sevenths."

I yanked him out of my way and pushed him back onto the bed. "I'm fucking serious. Look at this." I dangled the Blood Stone in his face. "What did you do to it?"

He blinked, looking genuinely surprised. "What did *I* do?" His wide eyes rolled to look at me. "Are you serious? You know I'm human, right?"

I released him and he rubbed his arm as if I'd bruised him. When I saw the yellow hue bloom across his arm, I realized that I actually had. "Sorry," I muttered.

He shrugged. "Comes with the supernatural territory, I suppose."

Feeling silly, I slunk back to the bathroom and pulled down the robe to wrap myself. Having nowhere else to go, I went to the bedside and slumped beside him.

Nate wrung his hands before speaking. "So, what do you think that means?" He looked down at his hands, his voice turning guilty. "Do you think it takes so much power not to feed on me?"

I froze. Did I seriously just drain my Blood Stone for a single night with a human? My eyes widened as I cradled the gem in my hands. Its light clearly was waning. This was all my fault.

"I could have used this to say goodbye to Sarah," I said, more to myself than to Nate. "I'd planned to, actually. When some time had passed and she'd grown used to…"

"Being human?" he finished for me.

I nodded. Tears sprung to my eyes. "I didn't know this would happen. I've lost my chance to say goodbye." The thought of never being with Sarah again broke my heart into a thousand tiny pieces.

As tremors began to overtake my body Nate wrapped an arm around my shoulders and pulled me in. "Hey now, it's all right. It's like those fancy batteries you get at the specialty store, it recharges, right?"

"Regular stores sell rechargeable batteries," I mumbled.

He chuckled. "Okay then. Bad analogy. But still, don't sweat it, okay? If it's all out of juice, you can just go talk to my dad and—"

I arched my neck to stare at him. Even he seemed to realize what he was saying and clamped his mouth shut.

I looked away as my cheeks began to burn. "Yeah," I said. "Great."

DEMONSPAWN DAUGHTER

Sonya

The one nice thing about being back home was that there were random closets filled with adorable outfits just my size. All the women in my family were five-foot-five, busty blonde beauties. I don't know if our race came with some kind of precoded DNA for what is supposed to be the sexiest womanly form, or if Hitler's Arian fanatics had a play in our creation —I wouldn't have been surprised. Either way, it felt damn good to take a steaming shower and open the closet in Nate's room, pull out a red skirt to accent my hips, a puffy white blouse to show off my cleavage, and red shoes to draw the eye down my long legs.

After slipping into the outfit like a favorite glove, Nate offered an approving appraisal before I went for the door.

"Babe," he said, waving his arms out in amazement. His outfit consisted of tousled hair and the sheets I had thrown at him, all too thinly draped over his perfect body. "Seriously, you can't dress all cute like that and then just leave."

I offered him a wry smile. "Really? You want to go again?" I popped open my locket and let him have a long look at the withering stone. "You want to test how much more it can take? I'm in if you are."

He stared me down, and for a moment I wondered if he was seriously considering the risk. Then he put on his classic jokester smile and crossed his arms, letting himself fall back into the bed with a dejected sigh. "Sucks to be human. You have no idea."

I chuckled and gripped the doorknob, feeling a mixture of pity and longing, which was an odd combination. When I closed my eyes, I saw images of Sarah, my past, and Luke, my future. Nate wasn't in there, and shouldn't be. There was no room for a human in my life. Especially not one who was the son of the Incubus King, the only person I knew who could help me recharge the Blood Stone. Talk about your fucked up love triangles.

When I slipped outside, Nate didn't protest. One quick glance before the door closed showed me his eyes closed, looking asleep in his bed. I wondered if this was as hard for him as it was for me. But as I clicked my heels down the empty hall, it felt silly to believe this was anything more than a stroke of good luck for him. How many humans got to fuck a succubus and live to tell about it? I was probably going to be the topic of his boyish bragging many drunken nights to come.

The best way to get over a guy, especially one who was just intended to be a one-night stand but had somehow turned into something more, was to have a distraction. I chuckled, realizing that Nate was *supposed* to have been my distraction. Well, it had worked far too well.

I still needed to get to Queens, but first I needed to deal with my grandmother. I turned a corner and found myself walking to the sunroom, knowing that's where she would be spending her morning tea if she was still the woman I remembered.

Sure enough, there she was sparkling like an orchid misted with morning dew sipping from a darling porcelain cup.

Her eyes crinkled with delight when she saw me approach. Nothing about her seemed aged except for her eyes. They were blue and bright, but ancient and ever-so-slightly wrinkled when she grinned. "Sonya, my sweet," she said, putting her tea on the table with a soft *clink* and rose to embrace me.

I couldn't resist falling into her arms, enveloping myself with her lilac scent and letting myself be lost in the embrace of a loved one. I didn't have any left, except her.

She nuzzled my face like a kitten. "I'm so glad you could find it in your heart to forgive me. I have missed you so much."

I squeezed her tighter. "Why did you do it?" I wanted there to be a good answer to the question. Why had she let me believe she'd been dead? I'd not only had to grieve my mother all alone, but grieve my grandmother too even when she'd been alive all this time.

She pulled away, her face scrunching with

regret. "I hated not telling you. But there was no choice. You never would have met *him* if I hadn't let you find your own path."

It was hard to swallow the lump in my throat. "What do you mean?"

She smiled, and then drifted about the sunroom trailing her fingers across the flowers. "Would you believe me if I told you?"

I frowned. "I've seen a lot of things. There isn't anything you could say that would surprise me."

She chuckled and wrapped her fingers around a rose just about to bloom. Her sparkling eyes found mine. "Your mother had a vision. She sacrificed herself to make that vision a reality, and if I had approached you before you met him, her death would have been for nothing."

Tears threatened at the edges of my eyes, burning like tiny embers. I swallowed and kept them in. "How could my mother have a vision? We're succubi. We don't have such gifts."

Her eyes drifted to the necklace about my neck and she said, "There are exceptions."

My hand went to it instinctually. The locket hadn't gone completely cold, meaning it still had some power left. What warmth I could feel spreading through my fingers made me feel solid and in control. "You're talking about Luke, aren't you?" I clenched my jaw. "Why does everyone think he's so damned important? I've tried looking for him, and he's supposed to be somewhere in Queens. Instead of taking me there, Nate and the random flight attendant dragged me here." I growled and stomped to a wicker chair, ignoring the small snaps as I jolted into the seat. "Why *deter* me from such an important task, as it were?"

She shrugged. "Your mother's vision made it clear the path would be set once you had met. After that, making it come true would be entirely up to you. Nothing I could say or do could interfere." She pointed her index finger in the air. "However, I'm not going to let a demonspawn drain your soul before I've had a chance to make amends."

I scoffed. "That sounds like you. Who cares about my safety, as long as you've made amends?" I narrowed my eyes. "Demonspawn," the word trickled off my tongue. "I thought they'd gone extinct."

She shrugged. "It was bound to happen again. They usually appear after the Blood Stone is recharged. I'm not sure why, though. It is odd." Her ancient eyes locked onto mine as if searching for answers. "You wouldn't know anything about it, would you?"

I froze into the best poker face I could pull off. I loved my grandmother, don't get me wrong. But I certainly didn't trust her farther than I could...well, farther than a human could throw a boulder. If she was talking about my daughter, I certainly wasn't looking to give away that secret.

Instead, I shrugged and reached for the pot of tea. An empty cup with two cubes of sugar was waiting for me. I cracked a smile. My favorite.

After pouring myself a steaming bit of tea, I swirled the mixture with a miniature metal stirrer and took a sip. I sighed. Absolutely heavenly.

My grandmother frowned. "Those monsters in Seattle obviously haven't been taking good care of you. When's the last time you had a decent cup of tea?"

I shrugged. "My whims have centered more around Oreos and beer, to be honest."

She drew the back of her hand to her forehead in a mock swoon. "My poor dear. What have they done to you?"

Cradling the warm cup in my hands, my mood turned somber. "If Luke is so important, what happens when I find him? Won't he just run from me like last time?"

"Is that his name?" She smiled as if I'd told her a dirty secret. "I'd always wondered."

"Seriously, Grandmother. He's not affected by my powers. What should I do?"

Her gaze fell to my locket again. "It seems the source of his fear is dwindling."

With my hand warmed from my cup of tea, I drew it up to the locket and was shocked that the metal felt cool and smooth against my touch. I arched my neck down and popped the locket open. It was nothing but a weak glimmer and the edge had turned white like an infection.

I swallowed hard against the lump in my throat.

One last rush of power, and my Blood Stone would be completely emptied.

I'd grown accustomed to the ease of which the Stone let me forget the price that came with being a Succubus. I could use my powers to excess, go months without feeding, and generally just live my life. But without it, I'd have to go back to how things used to be.

That thought rolled dread through the pit of my stomach which was already cold and heavy as I wandered New York's streets. The sun beat down, all too cheerful and the crowds of teeming people all too energetic for my melancholy mood.

The blood continued to drain from my face, making me feel faint as I thought about having to go back to my old life. How could I live like that again? Killing innocent men who'd pledged to die for me? No matter how I tried to justify it, pretend they were willing sacrifices, my powers took out all choice. They were nothing more than thralls, and I was no better than the Incubus King or Zack who threw away women like empty Cheetos bags.

The lust-filled glances ushered my way from more than a few men purposefully bumping into me down the street made me wonder if I should take my grandmother's advice to heart. Her words tore through me, "Live as you're meant to live. In the midst of life, and the only one who can drink the nectar." She didn't understand why I'd retained my brief whiff of human morals. She assured me it was youth holding me back, something I'd outgrow. She'd always touted morality to me, but that meant feeding on those who were willing victims. Old enough to know what that meant, it didn't seem so moral anymore.

As I wandered the streets, I realized I was approaching a familiar sight. In my mindless meandering, I'd come upon a church like the one in Seattle where I'd spent so much of my childhood.

There was one paramount reason I had any sense of morality, I realized with a wry smile. That darned nun, Maxine.

Still, I couldn't tear myself away from the magnetizing pull of the deep reds and blues of the stained-glass windows. Maxine had been a mother to me even more than my own had been. All I wanted was to feel safe and secure like I had with her.

Without thinking, I wound my way up the stairs and swept into the shadows of the church.

A sharp snarl sent my teeth clacking the moment I stepped inside, followed by a pained shriek just behind my ear.

I twirled and my skin went hot as I drew on the Blood Stone out of reflex. The girl who Nate had said was my daughter was just beyond the doorway and clutching at her hand which was already scabbing over with oozing blisters.

"Damn it, mother," she hissed. Her voice hardly seemed to match her teenager's body. The rumble of it was deep and angry, as if from a much older woman who had been screaming for hours on end. "Of all places, you decide to wander into a church?"

I stared at her, waiting for her to make a move. She retreated a few steps and the bubbles across her arm sizzled as a fresh layer of pink webbed over it. The wound completely disappeared and the pained lines in her face eased.

"Who are you?" I breathed. My senses were on full alert. My instincts screamed that this was a wild, cruel creature I had no business being around. No way should I let my guard down or dupe myself into believing I was safe. I gripped my locket and readied myself to drain the last of its power if necessary.

The silver shimmer of her eyes reminded me of Silvia, but there was a red tinge that burned around her irises that weren't from Silva, Derek, or myself. I realized there was only one place she could have inherited such a flame, the Blood Stone itself.

"Mother," she said again, as if I were being ridiculous. "You don't recognize me?"

She straightened as if she'd been sitting too long and rolled her eyes in a way that reminded me of a bored teenager. Yet, those red-ringed irises belied any sort of innocence.

When I didn't respond, she jerked her chin at the Blood Stone in my hand. "You clutch at that as if it's not a parent to me too. Do you really think it'd ever hurt me?"

My blood turned cold as she smiled. It wasn't the sweet smile of a young girl I'd expected with a face like hers. The pointy, slightly upturned nose and dimpled cheeks made her seem like a doll. But there was an ancient, evil element that seeped through her pores like a nightmare. I swallowed hard and took a step backward into the church.

She rolled her eyes again. "You can't stay in there forever."

"What do you want?" I snapped. "Why are you following me?"

She feigned a hurt expression by plumping out her bottom lip. "I wanted to see my mommy."

"No," I said, taking extra effort to make sure my voice didn't shake. "You aren't human. I didn't know what I was bringing into this world, what Silvia really is."

I could no longer deny what this creature was. This was a Demonspawn. A tremor rattled up my spine as I realized what Silvia must be in order to birth a Demonspawn. Where there are spawn, there are fallen angels.

"Fuck," I whispered under my breath. I slept with an angel? No...nothing so awe-inducing. I'd slept with a *fallen* angel.

Just as my Demonspawn daughter was about to make a witty comeback, she recoiled with a hiss as if she were a vampire exposed to sunlight. Not that vampires existed. That's ridiculous.

With a snarl she fled, the loops of her sleeves flinging with her as she vanished into thin air. I landed my hands on my hips and tilted my head with confusion.

"Your daughter seems lovely," a smooth voice caressed me from behind.

I swirled and was face-to-face with the object of my desire for the past three months. My eyes bulged and my jaw fell open. "Luke?"

He grinned and his whole face lit up in a way that made me want to grin too. His body was covered this time by a loose shirt, but the ripples of his abs were insinuated as a breeze flirted and tousled his hair. "You know my name," he said, sounding pleased.

I numbly nodded. "Of course. I've been looking all over the country for you."

For a moment, I just stared at him. His face wasn't flawless, as I'd expected. There were tiny scars that lined around his eyes and his lips, as if he'd been cut as a child. My fingers went to them of their own accord. "Why have you been running from me?"

"I wasn't running," he said, his eyelids lowering. His hand drifted over my fingers. "I visited my mother and then she told me to lead you here. So that's what I did." His gaze went distant and wary, staring where my daughter had just been. "Now I see why."

I blinked a few times. "That doesn't make any sense."

He shook his head and wrapped his fingers around my wrist. "We shouldn't talk about it here. Come with me."

My instincts told me not to trust him, but a rune that had long been cold ignited to life, reminding me that this was one of my four. I could trust him with my life. Sighing, I followed him into the shadow of the church.

Luke took me into the depths of steep halls that bent low into the ground, leading us down into the crypt where I expected creepy skulls and skeletons. It was New York, they liked those kinds of things.

We were stopped by a guard on the way down, but when he saw Luke's face, he nodded knowingly and let us pass.

"What's down here?" My voice came out hushed as if we were in a haunted place and I didn't want to disturb the spirits. It was a church, but it felt like something else altogether. It felt like we'd stepped out of reality and into a whole other realm.

Luke had no such apprehensions and his voice boomed, echoing down the corridor which looked suspiciously modern. "We're on holy ground," he said as if he'd invented the place himself and spread his arms wide.

I stifled a giggle and found myself already liking him. "Is that so?"

He nodded matter-of-factly and led me to a steel door which also looked terribly modern and ruined the creepy, ancient vibe of the place I was jiving with. "Didn't you see how demon-chick couldn't come inside?"

I narrowed my gaze. "Sure. But I also saw her run in terror when she saw *you*." A hint of distrust found its way into my voice. "Why was that?"

He shrugged as if women ran in absolute terror from him all the time. "Beats me." Without another word, he turned to the pad next to the door and pressed his thumb against it. The door unlatched and eased open with a hiss as if the room had been pressurized.

"Where the hell are we?" I demanded and resisted against his tug to pull me inside.

He gave me a sideways grin. "It's much easier if I just show you."

Curiosity battled with fear of the unknown. It hit me that no one knew where I was. I hadn't brought my phone. I was underground with my supposed soulmate, trapped inside because my Demonspawn daughter could be waiting to rip my throat out if I tried to leave, and now I was about to walk into a pressurized "holy" room with who knows what the hell else trapped inside.

Curiosity won and I found my feet echoing Luke's steps into the room which smelled like honey and roses.

ANGELSTONE

Sonya

A small crew greeted us once we'd made our way deeper into the bunker. They seemed familiar with Luke and didn't give me more than a curious glance. Half of them played cards while the rest exchanged glances over the tops of dusty old books, their phones lifeless black bricks on the granite countertops. I guessed bunkers didn't make good wifi hotspots.

Then I realized what was missing, what was striking me as odd and *wrong*. I wasn't sexually attracted to Luke, and nobody was even a little bit interested in me. They were all young men with thin t-shirts straining over bulky muscles like they were in some kind of photo shoot for hunks'a'licious. Which was immensely odd, because the stronger the male, the more he should be attracted to me, but after one look they'd all but lost interest. I jerked my locket from underneath my blouse and ripped it open. The stone still pulsed blue as it had before. It wasn't drained.

I closed the locket, still perplexed. Even if it had been drained, I was still a powerful succubus. These were all men ripe for the taking. What the hell?

"We can talk in here," Luke informed me. He waved me inside a dim room and seemed completely oblivious to my dilemma.

Unease sent bile up my throat. I slipped inside and was strangely grateful when Luke closed the door and we were alone. It unnerved me being around so many strong men I couldn't control with my pinky.

He gestured to the sitting area which was complete with decadent fruit and cubed cheese. I popped a grape in my mouth and tried to relax.

"I don't know what I am," he began, "but I'm not human."

"No shit," I murmured. "Sarah said you'd had

your heart ripped out and it fucking grew back. I sure hope you're not human. Otherwise you're Frankenstein's monster."

He snapped a grape from the vine and offered it to me, for the first time giving me a glimmer of attraction behind his sparkling eyes. "Do I look like a monster to you?"

I refused to take the bait and plucked my own grape from the platter, popping it into my mouth and chewing defiantly. "No. But I have a question," I said after I'd swallowed the morsel and deliberately ignored his question, "why lead me on a chase? You knew I was looking for you, right?"

He nodded. "You and everyone else. I couldn't trust you not to turn me over to that bastard you call your king." He snorted with disdain. "If you saw what he really looked like, you'd be fucking disgusted with yourself for ever sleeping with him."

"How do you know I slept with him?" I asked defensively.

He grinned. "I didn't until now."

I scoffed and leaned back into my seat. "Why'd you bring me here?" I demanded, flustered.

"I told you. My mother told me to lead you here. I didn't understand why until now. That daughter of yours had nothing good planned for you and it's my job to protect you from her."

"You didn't lure me here. I came on my own."

He chuckled. "Oh, really? I'm sorry, but no. I lured you with this." He held up a silver chain that glittered in the light. "It calls your destiny to you. I figured the muse would pick up on it. I made sure it knew I'd be heading to New York."

I went silent. So he knew our destinies were intertwined. Hearing him say it aloud was odd and personal, yet he didn't seem perturbed in the least. His eyes watched me, patient and kind. It wasn't as if he wasn't attracted to me. I could sense something there. But without the assistance of my powers, it was all a mystery.

"Why aren't my powers working?"

He shrugged. "There's no sex in heaven. It's a mortal's gift. It's meant to be fleeting and precious, just like any other mortal pleasure." He nodded to the walls. "This is a piece of heaven. A very tiny, minuscule piece, but enough to change the supernatural laws once you're inside."

I followed his gaze and scrutinized these so-called heavenly walls which were lined by seamless mirrors. Seeing nothing out of the ordinary, I bounced to my feet and made my way to the mirror. I grazed my fingers across the surface and gasped at the realization. It wasn't a mirror. It was a sheet of pure crystal, or was it diamond?

"What the hell is it?" I breathed.

He chuckled. "You're brazen to curse in the presence of angelstone."

"Angelstone?" I repeated the word as if that would help me wrap my mind around it. Then I registered that I'd just been insulted. "Who cares if I curse? It's just a word. Just a sound humans created to express distaste. It holds no meaning."

His jaw went taut. "Words are the most powerful thing in the universe. The entire cosmos was born by a single word. The stars, the ocean, life and death, were all born of *words*."

I had no response for such philosophy. What did I know of the creation of life and the universe? What did I care?

My fingers grazed the cool, silk sheet of angelstone. I found myself dropping my hand to my skirt and clutching the trim-line, my fingertips feeling chilled. I was never chilled.

I turned and shot him a playful grin. "A

gentleman is supposed to offer his coat when a girl gets cold."

Luke peeled off his shirt without hesitation and offered it to me. I chuckled. "I didn't mean the shirt off your back. That's a whole different level of sacrifice."

He grinned and dangled the cloth between his fingers. Even amidst the presence of angelstone, seeing his body again shot pleasure through me. Whatever had kept the air cold between us slowly melted, leaving something sweet and delicious on the tip of my tongue.

I approached to take his offering, grateful to have an excuse to examine his muscular physique. He was an amazing specimen. Most supernatural men had an agonizing level of perfection. Even Nate. I thought I liked that, until now. Luke's skin wasn't porcelain like a doll, but rough like a human's. The hairs on his arms were white as if he'd bleached them, and tiny scars lined his whole body. I found myself unable to resist the urge to trace my finger across some that were still pink, as if trying to heal.

"Detective Anderson's handiwork," Luke admitted.

I jerked my hand away, not realizing that I'd been stroking the outline of his abs. "I thought you healed?"

"I do. But a small mark always stays behind." His hand drifted to a red line up the center of his chest. "I prefer it that way. I never want to forget why I want to kill him."

Realization hit me. "Why are you on some blind mission to lead me to 'holy ground' by your prophetic mother? You should be tracking that bastard after what he did to you." And Sarah, I added in my thoughts.

He smiled. "Because the end of the world takes precedence."

"End of the world?"

God. I sounded like some blonde bimbo. Which in this case, I was.

"Yeah. It's real." His eyes fell to my Blood Stone. "And you're going to have to get rid of that, for starters."

My hands clutched it defensively. "Are you kidding? Do you know what this is?"

His cheeks pinched as if he'd tasted something bitter. "I know exactly what that thing is. It's entombed evil. It needs to be destroyed."

I shook my head. "Hell no! This is the only

thing that keeps me from killing people. Without this, I'm just a walking murder weapon and I can't do anything about it." My cheeks flushed with the unspoken certainty that I never would have experienced Nate without it, and he'd opened up a whole new world. One that questioned my desire to be with my so-called soulmate.

Luke's eyes narrowed, but he didn't make a move to snatch it from me. Instead the tension in his shoulders eased. For some reason, the pretense of "not giving a damn" made me bristle. I crossed my arms and shifted my weight to my hip. It probably made me look even more the blonde bimbo, but I was past the point of caring.

He snorted a laugh. "Look, don't get all prissy on me. We've got a lot to do."

"Like what?" I snapped. "All I'm interested in is making sure I don't need to kill people, which means either you help me or I go back to Derek and Silvia."

I wasn't sure what I'd expected to happen when I met my soulmate, but it wasn't this. He was supposed to fall madly in love with me, sweep me off my feet and nourish me with as much sexual energy as I could want. I wasn't supposed to have to go back to killing, or go back to bartering with the Incubus King to screw his wife and spawn demon babies.

Luke openly laughed at me, making my blood boil. "You already gave Derek what he wanted. You tipped things over to some dangerous dark scales by unleashing a Demonspawn on earth. Now they'll want your head on a pike. Your daughter is the first on the list who wants you dead."

Did he mean that literally? I sure hoped not. "Why would my own daughter want to kill me?" My words came out defiant, even though I'd seen the cruel gleam in the Demonspawn's eyes. She didn't look like she'd blink twice to lop my head right off my body.

Instead of responding, he gingerly sat on the plush sofa and reached under the maple table. A soft rustle sounded as he drew out a small box and cradled it in his lap. His face rose and his eyes met mine. The expression made me soften. There was something in his eyes I hadn't expected. There was hope, but also fear and dread. "It's better if I show you," he said, seeming to force the words out.

Suspicious, but curious, I eased into the seat beside him. "And that is…?"

His hand caressed the silver box as if it were the greatest treasure in the world. "Some would call it Pandora's box." He flashed me a grin. "To me, it's just the place I keep my soul."

My eyes dashed away from his magnetizing gaze. There was definitely attraction in it now. Electricity zinged in the air between us and my cheeks burned with the inappropriate thoughts that were springing into my mind. For some reason, I felt like Nate would approve of this. I could almost hear him in the background, telling me to get it over with so I could go share his bed again. "Sounds mysterious," I said.

He eased the chest open and my eyes were glued to the lid, dying to know what someone's soul would look like. To my surprise, a diamond rested inside. I chuckled. "Your soul is my new best friend."

He reached for me and my curiosity made me still. He took my hand and he guided my fingers to the stone's surface, closing his eyes as my skin grazed the glass. Emotions and memory surged after a moment of contact. I jerked, but his grip tightened, keeping my fingers pinned.

Memories infused me like a hundred ghosts taking claim of my mind. Images of a woman, fleeting feelings of being trapped in the dark. Crying. Torture. Detective Anderson ripping out my heart and then I was looking into my own eyes, frozen in a loop looking into my eyes, into my eyes, into my eyes...

The world snapped back to reality the moment my hand was freed from the diamond. I gasped for air and crawled to the other side of the sofa. "What the hell was that?" I squeaked. The memories continued to flood. They were incoherent and massive. My eyes darted as fleeting glimpses of shadows sprinted across my vision. My head jerked at every new voice that droned in the distance, every sharp cry of Luke's suffering at Detective Anderson's hands.

Then a deeper memory unfurled, one no human would ever remember. At first I thought it was one of the memories of Luke as a child, trapped in the basement when his mother had locked him away for "training." But Luke was much younger than that. Much, *much* younger.

I was inside a womb, just conceived by an angel father. No, not one... but three. Two angels and a... some supernatural I couldn't name.

Conceived with the power of a prophecy's blessing to combat the reign of terror that would come for this world. To save a conflicted succubus from darkness. To save the world from destruction. To save *me*.

The small room came back into focus. My eyes found Luke's and blurred with tears. "You're…" I couldn't say the word. It wasn't possible.

His eyes went wide and hopeful. "Did it work?" he whispered. "Only you can see what I cannot. Please, tell me what you saw."

I realized now why he wanted me to be linked to his destiny. It had nothing to do with romance or love. He simply wanted to know what kind of supernatural creature he was. He had no idea. Angels who hadn't fallen didn't breed, so how could he know he was one of them? How could he know that all the rules of natural order had been broken to conceive him in order to save the world?

Rage filled me the moment I realized his self-ishness. "How dare you!" I snarled and slapped my hand across his face as hard as I could. His face lashed to the side and his lip burst open, spraying blood across the floor. Being a succubus at full strength, he was lucky I didn't break his neck.

The sight of blood didn't deter my rage. I slapped him again, sending him sprawling to the floor. "How dare you force such magic on me without my consent!" I was angered he'd done something like that to me, but the truth was I was hurt. I had wanted him to love me. I'd wanted this fairytale of intertwined destinies to result in absolution and explosive, magical sex. I was wrong.

He groaned and tenderly wrapped his fingers around his dislocated jaw. He squeezed his eyes shut as he popped it back into place with a muffled cry.

I snorted. Served him right. The angelic bastard.

Without giving him a chance to recover, I stormed out of the room and down the hall back the way we'd come.

The men outside shot from their chairs the moment I smashed the final door open. I probably could have walked out without a fuss if I hadn't made such a scene, but I was pissed off.

A small glimmer of glee spread through my chest when they went for their weapons. They wanted to come at me? Fine, let them try. I needed an outlet for this rage.

My vision tinted in red as I drew from the Blood Stone. It was low, but it had plenty left to deal with these punks. Inferno spread through my limbs and filled me with energy.

The humans' eyes went wide.

One reached out his hand with disbelief. "This is holy ground," he said, as if to himself.

"So?" I smiled and drank in their delicious fear. "I'm not a demon. Just a succubus."

Recovering from their shock, the others readied their weapons. I crouched before launching myself at them like a bowling ball going head-first into a bunch of plastic pins. They scattered the moment I blurred into them, but not fast enough. I caught two by the belly, my fists putting the full weight of my momentum and force into the blows. They crumpled and I swiveled to deal with the last four.

Luke's lip curling into a snarl and a steel bat filled my vision before it bounced off my head and the world went black. The almighty succubus, wielder of the Blood Stone, soulmate to angels, taken out by a freaking *home run*.

IT'S NOT OVER

Nate

"What do you mean you don't know where she is?" my father's voice on the other end of the line roared. "Go find her, you idiot!"

If I'd thought the King's voice had been deafening, then hearing the silence engulfing me while knowing his unending rage was about to meet my face in a few hours was far worse. I couldn't do anything but keep the phone pinned to my ear as sweat ran down my neck long after the call had ended. The King was coming to New York? What would happen to me if I didn't have Sonya when he got here?

Panic rose in my gut like a swarm of bees and I forced myself to lower the phone and tuck it in my pocket. The room was dark and empty without Sonya in it, and I cursed myself for getting so attached to her after one night. But *damn*, what a night.

I readjusted my pants which strained at the zipper just thinking about it and began gathering my gear. I grabbed my heat-sensing goggles, my GPS tracker, and a small golden cross. Because, couldn't be too careful when a Demonspawn was on the loose.

A sharp knock at the door made me gasp and I clutched my chest. "Damn. What?"

The door cracked open and Sonya's grand-mother peered inside. I narrowed my gaze. I'd much rather be talking to Pete, the Incubus who'd gotten too close to the Demonspawn and aged like a mortal. He at least knew what we were dealing with. Not this ancient succubus who probably didn't give two shits about her granddaughter.

"I just wanted to check if you'd heard from Sonya," she asked. She was a powerful succubus, as any of the d'Ange family were, and I shook off the effects of her powers with a degree of effort.

"How the hell should I know? Sonya and I aren't that close."

She gave me a knowing smile. "My destroyed library would suggest otherwise."

Heat ran up my neck. "Yeah, well. She's not here."

She eased inside the room, shutting the door behind her. "I can see that."

Still organizing my gear, I retrieved my last but most important piece of equipment. My pistol.

The cool metal gleamed in the retreating sunlight from the draped curtains. I popped open the barrel and checked the rounds.

Sonya's grandmother didn't seem affected. If anything, she was more intrigued. I inwardly cursed myself. Of course a succubus would like a bad boy with toys.

"Calm down," I said with a smirk and kissed the pistol. "If a succubus is going to take my life, it's going to be your granddaughter."

She winked. "Of course. Let's go find her."

BAD LUCK

Lilith

The first time I'd seen my mother and that damned angelic bastard had ruined it.

"She hates me," I said to myself and pounded the heel of my palm into my forehead. "She fucking hates me!"

I allowed myself to scream with angst, then tried to rationalize my emotions. "Give yourself a break," I said into the mirror. "You're only three days old."

My green eyes and red-rimmed irises stared back. No way could I pass as human, no matter how I'd tried to change my appearance. I was a

Demonspawn. What use were my powers if I couldn't even decently hide effectively in public?

There was no way I could contain my rage, so I shoved my knuckles into the mirror and shattered it into a thousand pieces.

"That's bad luck for seven years," my father's voice said.

I rolled my eyes. "Shut up, *dad.*" I turned to glare at him. "What the fuck are you doing here?"

He clicked his tongue and eased into the room. "Such language. Don't be a bad girl."

I crossed my arms and glowered. "I'm a demon. I'm entitled to be bad."

He stroked my cheek and smiled. The fondness in his gaze melted away my rage. I knew he'd been desperately doing all he could to conceive me. My mother meant the world to him, and my father had done some pretty terrible things to make her his. I knew he'd do anything for me as well. "Sorry," I said, my shoulders lowering. "I'm just frustrated."

His thumb continued to stroke my cheek, but I saw his jaw tense. "Is it about Sonya?"

I nodded. "The angel's got her."

His hand fell and his flush of rage wafted through the room. My shoulders shot up to my ears again, but this time out of fear. I may have been a powerful and feared Demonspawn, but I was just a newborn. The Incubus King created me and could smother me out of existence with a snap of his fingers.

He must have gotten ahold of himself, because the room cooled and he shot me an apologetic glance. I relaxed. "That's all right," he assured me. His gaze turned to the window and he peered out over the city. I had a perfect view of the cathedral from here, the place where the angel had taken my succubus mother. I wanted to meet her, and I'd tracked her all the way here trying to do just that, but she was never alone.

I pressed against his shoulder and stared with him. "Do you think she'll come out?"

His arm wrapped around me and made me feel safe. "She has to, my daughter."

I didn't know his plans, but I imagined we had very different reasons to see Sonya again. My cheeks went hot and I refused to look up at him. He wanted something from her, and I was afraid it wasn't anything good.

HELPLESS

Luke

I felt like the biggest asshole to walk the earth. Sonya's limp body sprawled across the white marble floors and my uncles all watched me with expectant stares. They knew I was bringing a succubus into their territory, which was why they'd insisted I bring her here, to the fucking bunker of Angelstone. But now, seeing the purple bruise forming at her brow, I knew it'd been a mistake. She meant something to me that I couldn't explain. A connection stronger than heaven or hell spanned between us and stretched fingers out into the world calling to other pieces of my soul I'd thought lost. I couldn't let anything bad happen to her, but I was doing a bang-up job of that.

"What?" I snapped and rested the bat across my collarbone. "You wanted me to just let her beat you all to death?" The truth was, I'd been afraid for *her*. I kept my chin raised in defiance, hoping my uncles couldn't sense the truth. She was powerful, but the Angelstone would have drained her too quickly. My uncles were stronger than they looked. Even if she'd caught them off guard, they would have won in the end... and then she'd be dead.

"She needs to trust you," Uncle James said, breaking from the row of his brothers. They all looked my age, and if my mother hadn't warned me that they weren't human, I wouldn't have believed we could have been related.

"Yeah," I said, "you should have thought of that before you made me bring her here. The angelstone messed with her head."

Uncle James stomped up to me and laid a heavy hand on my shoulder, making sure I was looking him in the eye before he spoke. "Do you understand what's at stake, nephew?"

Before I could retort, the damn devil himself waltzed into the room.

"Well, well, well…" the Incubus King said as a smirk played across his flawless face. "Looks like you've made this easy for me."

My uncles reacted before I could, blurring and drawing the powers of the angelstone into their movements. I still didn't know what I was, if I was capable of more powers than just regenerating my flesh. I could do nothing but watch with awe as they did what they couldn't do with Sonya and went full-force against the Incubus King. His life wasn't important, and in fact, he was the enemy.

The angelstone affected him, but not enough to keep him from moving so fast he was a blur. He snatched Sonya from the ground and then a painful snap sounded as he broke my wrist.

"You're coming with me," he commanded.

I fought back with a snarl, trying to yank my limp arm free. Pain shot up my elbow but I ignored it, having been well trained by Detective Anderson's torture.

My uncles came after us, but they weren't fast enough. Pain blurred my vision as I was sped out of the cathedral's bunker and into the sunlight.

Away from the holy suppression of angelstone, the pain melted away and all I could feel was the intense desire to please the man with a death grip on my wrist.

He flashed me a smile, and glanced at my uncles swaying at the cathedral's doorway.

"Remember, Luke. Remember who you are!" Uncle James shouted.

The Incubus King hefted Sonya over his shoulder and I numbly followed. A part of me wished I knew who I was so that I had something to hold onto. Instead, the city's sunlight seemed to dim around the Incubus King and all I could do was follow in his footsteps, somehow feeling that my life was about to change in a terrible, amazing way.

CAPTIVE

Sonya

Raw desire woke me from my concussion-induced coma. Luke, naked and beautiful, peered down at me through the canopy of his eyelashes. His lust hit me like a blow and I curled onto my side, trying to douse the awakening of the second rune that recognized Luke as one of the four... but something was wrong.

We must have moved out of the range of angelstone, for the force of his lust pushed all thoughts out of my head. I'd never felt this drunk on lust before, except maybe when I'd been around the Incubus King.

I curled deeper into myself. Luke righted me and pressed my shoulders to the ground. He eased himself against my underwear. "I want you," he breathed. He moved, his erection rolling over my clit, sending pleasure awakening between my thighs. "I need you," he corrected.

A part of me liked being woken up like this, but it was strange. The Luke I'd gotten to know, however briefly, was in full control of his body. This one groaned like a madman, unable to think of anything but shoving himself inside me. Images flitted into my head, a rare extension of my powers when a man was fully invested in having me. It usually took weeks of preparation to get a man this engrossed into the fantasy that I could read his thoughts. Something was definitely wrong.

I battled against the force of lust, and his physical weight. He refused to lift away from me and his fingers grappled at my underwear. "Wait," I said, hesitating to enjoy his unexpected pleasure.

I held power over men, and their lust gave me life. Luke and I were meant for one another, we were meant to have sex that sent the stars reeling, but as his dick slipped under the fabric and squeezed through my body, I knew it wasn't supposed to be like this.

My head ached from the metallic bat that had rung my skull, the one that *Luke* had beamed me with. But I recovered from injuries with impressive speed, and sex only made my recovery faster. But this time, I wasn't able to drink in his lust. The sweetness of it kissed the air, but it lingered, as if it was something foreign and I had no knowledge of how to take it in. It slithered until it found my necklace and the heat of it burned my chest. Relief pricked my thoughts, glad that at least my necklace could drink what I could not.

Luke rocked against my body and I closed my eyes. I didn't know what would happen to an angel who fucked me. But why was he taking me? Where were we, if not in the bunker lined with angelstone?

I forced my eyes open and tried to gather a sense of my surroundings. Luke continued to groan on top of me, grabbing my breasts and squeezing. He was lost in the ecstasy, and a part of me wanted to join him. But there was no way I could shake the feeling of wrongness that lingered like a stench.

Then, I realized what it was. We weren't alone. My eyes found their silhouettes in the darkness, and I knew, without a doubt, that Derek, the Incubus King, was here. The form beside him I thought might be Silvia, or even my Demonspawn daughter. But when the light shifted and Nate's furrowed brow came into view, my breath hitched.

They watched in silence as Luke pummeled into me. I glared at the Incubus King, knowing that somehow he was manipulating Luke into doing this to me. Why would he want Luke to have sex with me? And why was he freaking watching?

When the Incubus King smirked, I shifted my gaze to Nate. His cheeks burned red and he cast his gaze to the ground, as if ashamed. Here was one of my four... standing by while Derek used me... used us. We were supposed to be a team. I didn't know how I knew that, but a voice inside of me screamed that Nate shouldn't just be standing there.

I thought they'd watch us the whole time until Luke was done. But Luke slowed, his eyes glazed over as if he didn't even know where he was anymore.

Derek scoffed and approached, resting his hands on Luke's shoulders. "Stop resisting. Finish it," he commanded.

The blue haze that drifted from his lips tinged Luke's nose. Luke's whole body convulsed and his dick throbbed inside of me, growing even bigger than before.

I hissed and snarled at the Incubus King. "What are you doing to him?" I demanded.

Derek ignored me, leaving us and Luke resumed his thrusts. I'd gone raw and groaned at the ache. I wasn't turned on by this; I was pissed off. My body wasn't complying to the supple wetness of enticement I usually enjoyed.

"There's got to be another way," Nate insisted, for the first time taking a step into the light and making my heart skip a beat that perhaps he hadn't abandoned me completely.

"You're the reason this is necessary," Derek retorted with a sneer.

I snapped my gaze to Nate and hoped that the question mark was painted across my face. What did he mean he was the reason?

The answer came with a burning heat that spread across my chest. Luke's passion flooded into me and this time, I couldn't help but groan with the sensation of his pleasure. His lust, no matter how forced, still found its way through my body and filled my Blood Stone, bringing it back to the fullness of life. Luke could power my necklace, and for some reason, the Incubus King wanted that to happen.

*A*fter a shower and a very, tender, moment of healing my raw skin with power borrowed from my Blood Stone, I wrapped a towel around my chest and made my way to Nate.

He was waiting for me in the bedroom, his face red with shame and anger. I'd never seen him like that before, and for a moment lost my resolve to rip him a new asshole.

"What the fuck was that?" I demanded.

Nate refused to look me in the eye. He stared at a spot on the wall and the muscles on his jaw rippled as he clenched his teeth.

I stomped to his side and gripped his chin, forcing him to look at me. His eyes were pained and it was difficult for me to keep his gaze.

"Nate, I need to know what's going on." To my surprise, my words were softer than I'd intended.

He peeled my hand from his face and wrapped his fingers through mine. His gaze fell to my necklace. "The angel would never have charged the Blood Stone for you without our intervention," he whispered.

I stiffened. "You know what he is?"

He nodded. "Derek told me."

Which meant he'd known all along who and what Luke was.

I growled and curled my arms over my breasts as I sat beside him on the bed, taking my turn to stare at the wall. "Why didn't Derek just charge it himself?"

Nate scoffed. "He'd need Silvia for that. And she wants nothing to do with him until Lilith has returned."

I peered at him from the corner of my eye. "The Demonspawn?"

He nodded. "Yes." He lowered and stared at his hands. "Your daughter."

I sighed. "Look, I don't know why he found it necessary to *force* Luke to fuck me. That was just messed up." I narrowed my eyes. "He's... important to me. I'm supposed to have sex with him, but not like that. I didn't like it."

He rubbed his forehead. "I'm sorry, Sonya. If there'd been another way—"

I punched him on the arm and he grunted. "Another way? There *was* another way! And why does he give two shits if I have a charged Blood Stone or not?"

He growled and shot to his feet. "Look, you proved that you can help him create Demon-spawn. He wants more." A shiver overtook his body. "He wants a fucking army."

END OF THE WORLD

Luke

*P*issed wasn't a strong enough word to describe how I felt. After finally gathering my uncles and luring Sonya to the bunker, I'd still lost everything.

I rapped the chain of my handcuff across the bed frame and tried not to let the rising panic take hold. After years of torture and imprisonment by one certified nutso named Detective Anderson, my mind was having a field day sending memories fluttering through flattened scars. I couldn't help but relive the agony of Anderson's blades slicing me open, his forceps ripping out my organs... his hand extracting my heart.

A soft hand brought me back to reality with a jolt. "Hey," a female voice whispered, soothing me.

I blinked and thought it'd be Sonya standing over me. The soft, sensual voice was so much like hers, and her touch genuine and kind. But when I saw those red-rimmed irises framed with green staring back, I reeled against my chains.

She lurched away from me, hurt flashing on her face. "Hey," she said again, this time the lilt in self-defense. "I'm not going to hurt you."

She hadn't sounded like this at the church. Perhaps the holy ground had damaged her voice box just like it'd sent boils across her skin. Or, perhaps, it exposed what she really was.

I snarled and she backed all the way to the window. "I'm not going to fall for your tricks," I snapped. She was going to curl her fingers over her elbows and act all innocent?

"There's no trick," she insisted. The sun supported her argument, filtering in its rays and making the green overtake the red in her eyes. With her round face, midnight curls, and bombshell boobs, she could have easily been a girl to fall in love with, not a hell-bound demon.

Sympathy filtered into her gaze. "I'm sorry for what my father is doing to you. I'd hoped to get Sonya away from him before he came." She frowned. "I didn't know I'd need to protect you, too."

I strained against my constraints and my wrist fought against the blister trying to form, my body continually healing. I wasn't going to question why this demon seemed to be on our side. Perhaps it was a trick, perhaps not. Regardless, she could give me answers. "What's the Incubus King planning?"

She shivered, but didn't leave her place at the window as the cold draft poured in. "The end of the world," she said flatly. And I believed it.

STAY ALIVE

Nate

"You've proven yourself untrustworthy," Derek declared.

I didn't want to hear it. This had been humiliating enough and I hated how powerless I felt. I'd seen the runes across Sonya's stomach and I'd been around supernaturals long enough to know a seer's prophecy when I saw one. No one liked to talk about it, but before I was born there'd been a disturbance strong enough to shake the supernatural community. Actual angels had come in legion, fought off some great darkness, then left as if nothing had happened. The story made its way around occult circles, which was one of my specialties. I learned things. Even as a human, I'd earned a name among supernaturals as someone who got shit done, who knew things I shouldn't know, and could keep a secret even if my life was in danger. I hadn't thought much of it until I'd felt the surge of power on Sonya's skin... power I was not supposed to have. I was human, or at least, I was supposed to be.

"Do you hear me, *boy?*" Derek spat.

I jerked my head up and met his glare. Let him think he had me. Even the Incubus King couldn't overcome destiny once it was activated. "What the fuck do you want from me, then?" I spat. "You have the angel. You have the succubus. Why are you even wasting your time berating me?"

Derek growled with warning and I took an involuntary step back. Pissing him off was probably a bad idea, but I was pissed off just as well.

"You, my son, are too attached to the succubus. I see the judgment in your eyes. Don't you know that a darkness is coming? There's only one way supernaturals will survive the coming wave."

I knew what he was talking about. The cycle of death came every thousand years and it took a psychic and her protectors to stop it. This time, something different had happened. An echo had broken through the realms, warning that something bigger and more terrifying was coming. There were more worlds than just the human world. There was heaven, hell, and the ghost realm. Rifts had started springing up all over the place, letting creatures in that weren't supposed to be here.

Derek knew all this, but what he didn't know was that Sonya was the prophet meant to stop it all from coming to fruition. She held the seven runes of power on her body... and one of them was linked to me, which meant I'd better stay alive.

"I'm well aware," I said, clenching my fists to keep the rest of the words from spilling out. I wanted to curse the Incubus King from here to Seattle and back. My fists shivered at my sides instead. "Just tell me my punishment so we can move past this."

Derek grinned, and it was never a good sign when he grinned.

Just hold on... just a little longer. There were

other runes on Sonya's body. Other souls that would make her unstoppable once she completed the unity of four.

I just had to hold on… and stay alive.

TO BE CONTINUED...

Continue Sonya's journey in Book 2: Siren Sins!

RECOMMENDED READING ORDER

All Books are Standalone Series listed by their
sequential order of events

Elemental Fae Universe Reading List

- Elemental Fae Academy: Books 1-3 (Co-Authored)

- Midnight Fae Academy (Lexi C. Foss)

- Fortune Fae Academy (J.R. Thorn)

- Fortune Fae M/M Steamy Episodes (J.R. Thorn)

- Candela (J.R. Thorn)

- Winter Fae Queen (Co-Authored)

- Hell Fae (Co-Authored)

Blood Stone Series Universe Reading List

Recommended Reading Order is Below

Seven Sins

- *Book 1: Succubus Sins*

- *Book 2: Siren Sins*

- *Book 3: Vampire Sins*

The Vampire Curse: Royal Covens

- *Book 1: Her Vampire Mentors*

- *Book 2: Her Vampire Mentors*

- *Book 3: Her Vampire Mentors*

Fortune Academy (Part I)

- *Year One*

- *Year Two*

- *Year Three*

Fortune Academy Underworld (Part II)

- *Episode 1: Burn in Hell*

- *Book Four*

- *Book Five*

- *Book Six*

Fortune Academy Underworld (Part III)

- *Book Seven*

- *Book Eight*

- *Book Nine*

Crescent Five *(Rejected Mate Wolf Shifter RH)*

- *Book One: Moon Guardian*

- *Book Two*

- *Book Three*

Dark Arts Academy (Vella)

Ongoing serial

Unicorn Shifter Academy

- *Book One*

- *Book Two*

- *Book Three*

Non-RH Books (J.R. Thorn writing as Jennifer Thorn)

Noir Reformatory Universe Reading List

Noir Reformatory: The Beginning

Noir Reformatory: First Offense

Noir Reformatory: Second Offense

Noir Reformatory Turns RH from this point with the addition of a third mate

Noir Reformatory: Third Offense

Sins of the Fae King Universe Reading List

(Book 1) Captured by the Fae King

(Book 2) Betrayed by the Fae King

Learn More at www.AuthorJRThorn.com